ZAYLAN FLYNN

To Be Damned

Copyright © 2023 by Zaylan Flynn

All rights reserved. No part of this publication may be reproduced, stored or transmitted in any form or by any means, electronic, mechanical, photocopying, recording, scanning, or otherwise without written permission from the publisher. It is illegal to copy this book, post it to a website, or distribute it by any other means without permission.

This novel is entirely a work of fiction. The names, characters and incidents portrayed in it are the work of the author's imagination. Any resemblance to actual persons, living or dead, events or localities is entirely coincidental.

Zaylan Flynn asserts the moral right to be identified as the author of this work.

Zaylan Flynn has no responsibility for the persistence or accuracy of URLs for external or third-party Internet Websites referred to in this publication and does not guarantee that any content on such Websites is, or will remain, accurate or appropriate.

First edition

Cover art by Zaylan Flynn

*This book was professionally typeset on Reedsy.
Find out more at reedsy.com*

Contents

Playlist	v
Map	vii
The Stranger	1
Arabella: I need to be able to breathe	3
Aerilyn: Home sweet Home, I suppose	7
Valin: Name Day Celebration	11
Aerilyn: Everybody wonders what it would be like to love you	13
Val: Change is never good	19
The King: Decisions	23
Arabella: A new competitor	26
Aerilyn: Make me	31
Arabella: Confessions of a Princess	35
Valin: That Damned Temptress	39
Arabella: Meeting the competition	43
Aerilyn: That inevitable Day	52
Arabella: When darkness comes	57
Arabella: These feelings	61
Valin: Damned Temptress	68
Arabella: Feelings	74
Arabella: Ball of Nightmares	79
Valin: Night Alone	84
Aerilyn: Practice makes Perfect	90
Aerilyn: Now Is the Time	95

Valin: Thank you	98
Aerilyn: I understand	104
Arabella: Champion	108
Arabella: Name Day Celebration	111
Valin: Chokehold	118
Aerilyn: Caught in Feelings	123
King: The Seer	133
Arabella: Captured	135
Aerilyn: Focus	139
Valin: Blood of Blood	141
Aerilyn: I wanted you both	147
Arabella: The Aftermath	149
Arabella: A Royal wedding	153
Aerilyn: Selfishness	163
Arabella: No time for goodbyes	169
Aerilyn's Father	173
Bonus: Arabella: Heart Desires	175

Playlist

1. Lilith by Halsey, Suga
2. Breathe by Fluerie, Tommee Profit
3. Willow by Taylor Swift
4. Running With The Wolves by Aurora
5. Gold Rush By Taylor Swift
6. Familiar Taste of Poison by Halestorm
7. Young and Sad By Noah Cyrus
8. Running up that hill By Halocene
9. Make Me… by Britney Spears
10. Until I found you By Stephen Sanchez
11. Eat Your Young by Hozier
12. Still into you By Paramore
13. Ghost By Justin Bieber
14. Never Be Me by Miley Cyrus
15. Wash It All Away by Five Finger Death Punch
16. I can't go on without you By Kaleo
17. I Want More By Shawn James
18. Are You Really Okay By Sleep Token
19. Everything has changed By Ed Sheeran, Taylor Swift

20. The Hills by The Weekend
21. Lost on You By LP
22. The Purge By In This Moment
23. Let me Love you Like a Woman By Lana Del Rey
24. Take what you want from me By Post Malone and Ozzy
25. Rewrite the stars By Anne Marie, James Arthur
26. Francesca By Hozier
27. Chokehold by Sleep Token
28. Go easy on me By Adele
29. Hate to be lame By Lizzy McAphine, Finneas
30. Bad Dreams By Bellhound Choir
31. Everybody wants to rule the world By Lorde
32. Diamond Heart By Lady Gaga
33. Kings Never Die by Eminem ft. Gwen Stefani
34. Wrong by Zayn, Kethlani
35. She Used To Be Mine By Sara Bareilles
36. Dynasty By Miia
37. Save Yourself By Kaleo

Map

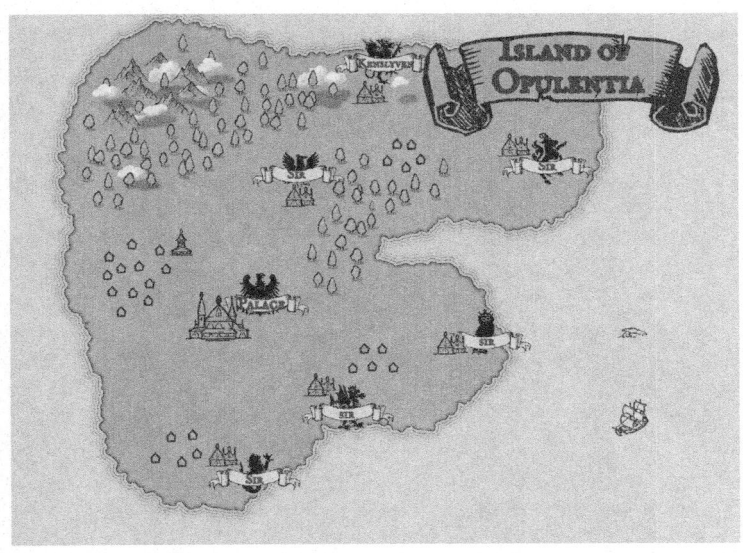

The Stranger

I awake to the smell of smoked meat and the sound of celebration. The noise is ridiculously loud. It has been years since I had left my cave, but I had to find out the source of my disruptive slumber.

Magic is second nature to me. Calling forth an easy disguise to blend in with people's masses. Simple pants and Tunic with a cloak always seemed to be fine. I don't know how long I was asleep, but I hope it was not so long that I look too out of place.

Coming down the mountain proved to be difficult with human legs, but after my last encounter with the people of Opulentia, they thought they had slain me. It is better they continue to believe that. When the knight had driven his sword in my chest, I had half a thought to go back and burn the rest of the Kingdom, but when I looked down at it I seen her ghost prints of places she liked and I could not bring myself to burn her away.

They filled the City with people dancing and drinking. Entertainers in the middle playing loudly. I am not sure a single one was sober enough to play a decent note, or if I was just too upset to be alert. I look up at the podium and see her sitting there on her own throne. It seems to be a celebration of her name day. I watch her from the shadows. Lost in time, I watch her. Lost long enough, the sun was starting to set until someone came around lighting the oil lamps.

I knew at that moment I had to have her. Not because of the status she carried nor for the beauty that was evidently there.

I have to have her because she looked so much like her. The way she walked and carried herself. Like she had no care in the world and the world would never break her. The way she smiles and the candles illuminate just a bit more, like soldiers standing at attention for their queen. Her eyes. Her eyes held the same wonder and secrets as *hers*.

Her eyes looked just like *hers*. It was almost like I could see her soul in this young woman. When the moment arises, I will have her. I will make her mine.

Arabella: I need to be able to breathe

The sun is shining bright today. I stare out of the window hoping to get a good glimpse of the town, but the walls and trees around the castle prevent us from seeing past it.

My mind wonders to what the people are doing. I sigh, wanting to be able to go out and meet them. The door to the throne room opens and my father's advisor walks out, looking up at me uninterestedly.

"Your father will see you but only for five minutes. Then he has an important meeting with the council to go to," he states and walks back into the room. I follow behind closely, doors shutting closed behind as I enter. Once I step in front of my father, bowing in respect.

"Good morning father," I greet. He smiles at me and kisses my cheek softly.

"Good morning, sunshine. What can I help you with?" He asks. The back of my throat felt dry. Clearing it, I try to get the confidence to speak.

"I would like to go beyond the walls of the castle, father. I want to meet the people to listen to them." Feeling my heart racing, I hold my tongue when I see my father sigh. It's not the first time we have had this conversation and I could see the dismissal in his eyes.

"Arabella, you are safe here. These walls protect you. We cannot risk your safety," he explains.

"But what does it mean to be safe when the people haven't seen you in years? They do not respect me as a princess because I haven't shown my face in front of them. You've seen the newspapers. Some of them believe I died years ago, and you have hidden the truth from them. The rest won't respect me and will not respect me once I become queen," I argue.

"They don't need to respect you. When you have a husband, he will be the next king. He will take care of all of that," His eyebrow twitching in agitation.

"But why should me getting a husband and a new ruler please them? Why can I not learn what the people want? Learn what they need and help them?" I look up at him. His expression unreadable. There was a silence for a moment and then father sighs.

"Arabella, it is not something you need to concern yourself with. Your job is to find and choose a husband. He will then work to make this country good to keep them safe," he explains, and I shook my head no.

"I am so tired of feeling like I'm a bird locked in a cage father. I understand you want to keep me safe, but keeping me locked up in here isn't helping me! I'm doing everything you ask of me. I will oversee the competition. I will choose a man to marry to please you, but please, let me out of the castle walls!" The tears were falling down my cheeks at this point. The

Arabella: I need to be able to breathe

room was silent. The guards look uncomfortable at where this conversation was going. My father's hand rubbed his forehead as if this conversation was giving him a headache. I squeeze my fists tightly by my sides, trying to keep it together.

"You will not go beyond the castle walls, Arabella. That is final." His voice rang with authority. His word was absolute.

His voice is raised, which was rare for him. He was always so calm when he talked to me, but this was different. I slowly took a step away from his throne. The walls felt like they were closing in on me and my breathing became labor. I bow my head at him quickly and turn around.

I gather my skirt and run out of the room. I heard footsteps running behind me to keep up and I knew it was Valin. Ever since he has been posted as my guard, he hasn't left my side.

I run into my room and the sobbing starts. I felt like I couldn't breathe and my lungs were grasping for any oxygen it could not find. Feeling hands on my cheeks forcing me to look up. Meeting the gaze with the worry eyes of Val. He was saying something, but everything was muffled, almost as if I was under water.

"Jesus princess! Breathe!" He shouts. Moving his body, showing himself taking slow, deep breaths. I copy what he was doing. After a few seconds, my breathing calms and I was left with only the tears falling down my cheek.

Valin wraps his arms around me protectively. In return, I wrap my arms around his waist tightly, my face in his chest. He strokes the back of my hair gently, as if I was made of glass that was ready to break any moment. I wasn't far off.

"I feel trapped Val, this castle is big but to me it feels like its closing in on me. I can't do this anymore," I cry and felt him squeeze me tighter to him.

"I promise, princess, I will find a way to make sure you're safe enough to go out there and see your people." This was the first time he dare put his arms around me. I know he was only doing it to calm me down, but I felt as if I was melting into his embrace.

And as much as I wanted to believe that he would find a way to help me. A part of me wondered if it was even in his power. But I didn't say anything. I let him hug me close to him against all protocols because it felt right; he felt right.

Aerilyn: Home sweet Home, I suppose

Behind the small Kenslyven palace is heavily wooded, and I am about to sneak out to explore it again. I was always told stories when I was younger about how it is filled with dangerous creatures, ghost and witches. No one has personally seen the creatures. The ones that told the stories, that is.

I am a very curious person, and I had to see for myself. The first time I was caught, I was given a lecture on obedience. The second time I was sent to the Royal Palace. If I was to believe in witches, that would have been then. The princess had bewitched me. Bewitched everyone at there and she acted as if she had no idea. We were both young girls, but her honey hair with natural waves was eye-catching. Her blue eyes looked deep almost as if you looked too long you might be about to see the treasure buried within them. We clicked right away. I felt if we did not, I would have become obsessed with being the person she would like. Maybe I was.

Every year for ten years, I came to see her for the summers. I looked forward to them. Out of no where though they stopped two years ago, after my mother passing. It was easy to go unnoticed. I had no desire to leave. Finding myself hoping that ghost were real. Just in the hope of seeing her on the palace grounds or even in the woods. I never saw her, but I found myself sneaking out to the woods. Sneaking was a strong word though. No one noticed me gone as long I was there for breakfast with my father on Sundays. Those are the holy days. We eat breakfast and go to mass until noon. Then I am back to being invisible.

Now that is how I am here, slipping out the back door with a bag with a few snagged bread loafs and my book. The sun was high, but the clouds were low so I think I had a few hours to explore before it became so dark I wouldn't be able to see. I thought I had explored everything, but I heard one scout raving about a witch and 'the hags cottage'. I had stumbled on an abandon cottage a few years back and found the book I carry around now. It was not a bad book but it would completely be considered a witch spell book, but it was just an herb book. A practice in mixing herbs to help sick or injuries.

I tried to go back the following day, but I must have had forgot where it was because it was not there. That was two years ago and now I know how to read a map. The map I may have stolen from my father's study. Following the directions and mark of the map, but when I got to the spot, it was not there. I walk around in circles. I found many herbs, that I pick but no cottage was seen.

The fog was still very thick and between it and the thick pine trees; it was becoming hard to see. Maybe the sun was setting, but I couldn't be for certain. Not with the low clouds. Discouragement was setting in and decide to head back.

Aerilyn: Home sweet Home, I suppose

I hear the howling of dogs and talking start to get louder as I get past some of the tree clearing. The backyard was filled with scouts and servants and they were all turned, looking at my father. As I seen him, his eyes lift meeting my gaze. Fear was there first and the once realization washed over him there was nothing but anger.

"Glad to have you back, Aerilyn." I hear him yell. The crowd of people turns at his words and start to part a trail that led to my father. I had half a mind to turn and run back to the woods. My father was dressed in his usual black attire but he stood on a wooden box which made him feel even more of a threat that loomed over me. Two scout men stood on either side of him. "Care to elaborate where you disappeared to?"

"I just went for a walk. There is a small clearing that I sometimes like to sit in." I try to brush it off. I can hear the stir of murmurs and the people moving about their day now that I am back. "Are you feeling well, Father? It is not Sunday?" I stop just before him as he steps down and meets me eye to eye.

"We have been called to the royal palace."

"Arabella?" Her name sounds like a stranger on my lips but I can not help to smile. The thought of seeing her again makes my heart hum.

"Hm, yes, the princess. They have invited everyone to celebrate a tournament in her name, the prize being her hand." He muses.

"Marriage? Already?" I could not hide my surprise. I knew this day would come even for myself, but it felt too soon.

"Yes, maybe I will be able to find you a suitor also. Take on the opportunity that has been handed to us. Go pack. The carriage will be ready soon." I gather my dress and only make it a few steps before my father grips my forearm. "Aerilyn before you leave, hand over the map that you took from my office." I do so, not giving him excuse him to go through my things and leave before anything else could be spoken.

Valin: Name Day Celebration

I had spent some time making a plan. Thoughts of trying to please the princess were never anything new. I remember her words from the other day crying over her conversation with her father. The day I went against every rule about touching the princess and holding her.

I had placed a request to meet with the king. I did not expect him to be so willing to see me immediately. Knowing he would have seen me if I called a council meeting, but I need not the opinions of dusty old men to sway what I was trying to get done. I knew it would have been a long shot, but I brought up enough security to get him to say, yes.

I walked into his chambers, and he looked to be sipping on scotch. By the smell of it that's what it seemed to be.

"Good Evening, Majesty." I gave a bow.

"Valin, You asked to speak. Why?" He gestured for me to sit in the chair in front of him. I took a seat and place the file I had on the coffee table.

"I did. I did not expect you to see me at this hour. I could have waited until the morning." I offered but knew what his answer would be.

"Nonsense, They said it was about Arabella."

"Yes," I laid out the plans and explain the line up. "You see sir. She would be well guarded. Nothing will happen if all goes to plan. Plus it is the last day of the tournament. So it should be nice to have one night with her people."

"You are sure, no harm would come to her."

"Indeed, Your Majesty."

"I know she feels trapped." There was a deep sigh that escaped him. "Fine, you have my blessing. Move forward with it. Surprise her with it. You are in charge of directing it." I gave him a bow.

"Thank you Sire." I said. He just waved me on. Dismissing me.

Aerilyn: Everybody wonders what it would be like to love you

The carriage ride was long and painful. The need to get there before the sun falls seems to be of utmost importance. I think because of the nasty rumors of increasing numbers of road bandits. If there was any, there would be more with the call of royals gathering. The call for everyone interested in the hand of the princess. Which meant people with titles and money would be gathering. A gold mine for the bandits.

The princess's hand was something everyone wanted, including me. If only I was born a man and I might have a chance. Stupid society with their stupid rule. The stupid need of a stupid heir. The bloodline needs to continue. Seeing as there was no male heir and she was an only daughter, she must marry.

I remember late-night talks. How she was a hopeless romantic for a knight in shining armor riding on a white horse. She was a princess but she was far from locked in a tower even if she felt that way.

I recall some of the letters she had sent me in the years of dealing with the death of my mother. The changes of a personal guard were always posted. How she felt trapped. How the check-in on her whereabouts became a hassle to go anywhere freely. There was always a lot of complaining but in the end, some positively hopeless romantic notions that would come of her situation.

I kept all the letters. Even if I could not find it in my spirit to write back. I knew I had nothing that would be heartfelt because in those days they had become cold. But reading her letters kindled the small fire in the depth of the night. So I held them close to my heart on days that felt the coldest.

The cool window of the carriage was nice as I leaned my face on and watched the sunset. The line of trees turns into fencing and open green hills. We getting close and the pain of sitting in this damned thing was becoming unbearable. Sitting alone in one of these things this long was incredibly lonely.

The slow buildup of feeling the bumps of the dirt roads turning to cobblestone was like music to my ears. The fencing turns to buildings and homes. We had entered the kingdom, Opulentia. There were flowers, petals, and streamers strung. The decorations were set up just for the princess that they loved so dearly. The princess seemed completely oblivious to what people thought of her.

I sit up and straighten myself. I fix my hair and make sure my clothes are patted out. It had been years. I wanted to look as good as possible. I wanted her to see me. *Why?* The thought started to plague me. It was not like she and I could run off into the sunset together. I just had to know. To know if she ever felt anything for me like I felt for her. If the thought of me invaded space in her thoughts like me.

One could just outright ask but it is so easy to let a lie slip off the tongue. Maybe the day would come that I would but I do not feel like breaking my heart tonight when I see her. I had a week. One week to test the waters. One week before she was to marry I then courted by a suitor of my father's choosing. I could make one week the best, right?

There was a sudden stop with the horses. I dare myself to take a glance behind the curtain windows. The stairs that led to the main entrance of the castle were just as grand as I had remembered it. The curved stairs looked like a current that drew people in. The embellishments of gold in the swirl patterns. The stones were so polished that it was white.

The footman opens my door and places a wooden step for me to easily step out. I take his hand. There was a line of carriages behind ours. I made a quick movement to follow the servant who had my luggage. I walked the walk, the stretch after spending the whole day sitting in that awful contraption.

At the top of the stairs, the doors were held open. A purple-lined rug that led to another set of stairs. There were several servants running around like bees in a honeyhive. I found myself leaning toward the servant with my things.

"Do you know where I will be staying?" the man slowly nods.

"Everyone's room has been made in preparation. I will be taking your things there now. So if you would like to follow me, I will show you." He did not falter his steps and began to step up the stairs. The stairs split off into two spirals. One spinning left and the other right.

I don't say anything but I do follow him. He walks up the stairs and walks to the right side. They seemed to twist a few times before revealing a dark hallway. The hallway was illuminated lightly with candles and the curtains were drawn back but the sunset did not give much light.

He turns left and there were several doors. All the doors seemed to be rounded and thick. With detailed designs of flower patterns. The hallway started to turn and there was a single door before there was another set of stairs that led down. We did not go down the stairs though, The last door, he opened with one hand.

The room was large, filled with furniture, lavious rugs, and pillows. A fireplace with a lounge and coffee table to the right. On the left of them was a huge bed with a bathtub on the other side of it. The room was decorated with colors of red and light greens.

The servant lays the luggage on the bed. He turned towards me and gives a slight bow. He sits back up, his hand still over his heart.

"Anything else, your grace?" His eyes met mine.

"Yes, where can I find the princess at this time of day?" I look back to the window and back to him. "Uh, evening." I corrected.

"The parlor." He said making a quick move to lower and then left swiftly.

There was a vanity along the wall of the window. I move to it and fix my hair. There were a few flyaway strands that I put back in place. I stood up looking in the mirror and made sure to red dress was not in wrinkles.

The material moved as I look. The lace was laid perfectly showing off my slender shoulders and just a small amount of cleavage. I pick a few lints off and made my way out of the room.

I make my way down the hallways and down the stairs. The

Aerilyn: Everybody wonders what it would be like to love you

downstairs was just as busy as it was when I first got there. I look left and right. There is a set of double doors leading to two rooms. One on the right looks like the dining room and the other looks like a parlor room. The room was full of people. Between servants, men and women. The volume of the growing chatter was almost overwhelming. But I walk in.

Many people were holding champagne glasses. There were a few lounges by the fireplace next the piano. There were a few girls sitting but in the middle, I saw her.

There was a subtle glow around her pink dress. The color of youth and adventure. She was so full of it and it shows in just her smile alone. She had grown so much since the day I last left the castle. Her long blonde hair was neatly braided into a crown. The small dainty crown was replaced with something with a bit more diamonds. The flush from her cheeks matched the color of her dress.

I was magnetized to her, Arabella was a surviving rose in the dead of winter. Everyone around her begged to pluck her from the deep snow. Her eyes scan the room while she was laughing about something someone told her.

The moment her eyes found mine, the smile that was invading my face was inevitable. The gentleman in front of her took her hand and place a gentle kiss. Her eyes broke for a brief moment. Her lips found the words, 'Thank you' and then she rose.

She looked like she was about to run but remembered all eyes were on her. The act of being a lady was one that was to be upheld, even more so in times like this. I met her halfway. Taking her gloved hands into mine.

She looks up at me. She was not much shorter than I am now. But short enough I could lean down ever so slightly and met her lips to mine. I chase the thoughts as she takes a deep breath.

"You made it," The words she spoke were like a melody to my ears.

"Did you think I wouldn't?" I gave her a subtle smirk before bringing her hand that was just kissed to my lips. It was the softest touch but I could have sworn I heard her quietly gasp. There was a playful smack as she jerks her hand back.

"You don't write anymore. How was I to know?"

"I am sorry. I will make it up, I promise." She pulls me in a hug. I take in the deep smell of rose and citrus that she seems to carry.

"I am just happy to see you. You must sit by me during dinner."

As she pulls back from the hug, I let my lips brush across her cheek.

"Whatever you wish, Arabella. I better make myself scarce in the meantime. But let me tell you, you look as beautiful as a pink rose tonight." I found myself unable to meet her eyes and left to find some wine to help me calm my nerves.

Before I could take two steps, I ran into another person. I go to give an apology only to see a gentleman. He had dark curls and deep forest-green eyes. There was a level of ruggedness with his stubble around his chin. I then noticed his guard uniform. Before I could say anything, he looks past me. I follow his gaze and see the princess leave the parlor and him brushing past me to follow her.

I blink after them. Not able to process what I had seen. I felt as though I met this man before. I mean he wore the knight's uniform so I am sure I had but there was a sense of familiarity. I just could not place my finger on it.

Val: Change is never good

I did not mean to run into the duchess. Maybe a part of me wanted an excuse to see her. Just to see how much she had changed. I could tell she did not recognize me. A part of me was relieved.

Some things did not go unnoticed, though. Her childish figure was now gone. She was slightly taller. Her brown hair even pinned, I could tell was longer. Her big brown doe eyes still screamed innocence even though I knew was foolish. She still had that terrible habit of biting that pouty lower lip.

I left when I realized I had been looking at her too much. I told myself it was natural. That came with the job. Taking in every detail to know who was getting close to the princess. I could not deny the stir of desire when I saw her bite her lip, though.

I follow the princess when I saw she had taken off. She gave a quick glance, not seeing me before leaving. She thinks she is sneaky, but I would never leave my eyes off her for long. Even more so now, with all the people coming into the kingdom.

Granted, they seemed to be of some royal status, but that did not mean they all had good intentions.

Her pink skirt flowed behind her as she made it out to the gardens. She took off her flats and wiggled her toes into the glass. She made it to the fountain before I had caught up to her.

"Needing the air, princess?" I kept a few feet paces back with my hands kept behind me. I held them back there to give a sense of informality.

"Oh, Val. Yes. There are a lot of people here." She started to walk around the fountain.

"Yes, you did see the list before they were sent? I thought I brought them to you." I follow but make sure to keep my distance like always.

"I did but seeing everyone under one roof is a little more overwhelming than I thought it would be." She pauses her walking and it takes everything in my power not to reach out and touch her. The small wisp of hair fell out of place. Touching her shoulder. It would be so easy to move it, to glide my fingers over the exposed flesh.

"Are you okay though?" I let my thoughts wander but not her honor.

"Yes, I think I just needed some air. A walk. Before super."

"We can walk the maze if you want?" I knew every turn by heart just as she probably did. But her thoughts never went where mine did. Memorizing every secret place. A secret place that would allow me to corner her. To grant me the chance to taste her lips. Those were dreams of course. Dreams that I welcome every night when I bid her goodnight.

"I think I am fine now. Thank you, Valin." She walks up to me and pats my shoulder. I freeze at the contact. I can't help

Val: Change is never good

myself. I want nothing more than to take that hand into my own. She walks by towards the palace again.

"I think I will stay here for a moment longer. I will follow you in there." I give a small bow. "Princess."

"Okay, I've told you before. You don't have to be so formal. You can call me Arabella." She leaves before I answer and call her princess again. But I hold my tongue until she is out of earshot.

"Yes, Arabella," I whisper to myself to hear in the darkest part of the night.

I sit on the side of the stone fountain and touch my shoulder where she touched. I thought working through the ranks would be enough. To spend every day possible protecting her. I wanted it to be enough.

We all knew this day would have come. The day she would need to choose who to marry. It was not like she needed to marry for political gain so there was no pressure there but she had not chosen yet. She would not choose so there was no surprise to this competition coming upon her.

I know she does not like it but what choice did she have left? The thought of her marrying someone other than me made my blood boil. How would I know if they treated her right? What if this new husband dismissed my position and there would be no one else to protect her?

I felt the night cold air was starting to seep in through my uniform. I stand up. As I stand I made a decision. I was going to throw my name into the competition. She may not love me like I have fallen in love with her. I would never push my love on her but I can make sure she would be protected. I would make sure no ass hat forced themselves on her.

I decided all those years ago in that wildflower field that I did not want to leave her side. I drove that nail in after that last attempt of kidnapping that happened after her sixteenth name day.

Who it was that attempted it was not found or caught. For I knew that person was here.

I walk up the stairs into the palace. The chatter of the people merged to the other side as they all started to congregate in the dining room. I see Arabella sitting at the left of her father along with Aerilyn sitting on the other side of the princess. The Duchess was smiling so brightly and only had eyes for the princess. I couldn't blame her.

I see a shadow move from the corner of my eyes. There was a window that peaked in directly in front of the princess and I could have sworn I saw something move outside of it. I take a closer look and see the bush is moving, but no sign of anyone else's presence. I hoped for it to be a play of lights, but I would only feel better once I got a chance to walk the perimeter once I was relieved from duty tonight.

The King: Decisions

The morning sun was streaming into the council room. I had my back sitting away from the sun, but the warmth of the summer morning was comforting. I see all my closest men sitting around the table looking at me. Seeing their confused faces, they wanted to know why I called a meeting.

I have been holding a lot of meetings. A lot of them, not even me calling the meetings. There was a pressing threat that we were trying to keep from the people. The people and my daughter. She was always so naïve and kind. Even after the attempted kidnap, she was oblivious to the dangers that could have happened.

To her and the people that was the one and only danger that was happening right now. We were always a little out of sight on our own island. Self-sufficient. Having our crops and healthy animals to keep the people fed. We were blessed.

Blessed. The people here served the god, Alos. Ever since I was a boy. I could not tell you if this god was real but I was not about to be the one to break the people's faith or break what has been working for hundreds of years.

Thoughts of my daughter's words came to mind. I know she felt trapped but there was nothing I could do for her. The best solution I had with all that was going on was to get her to marry. The people needed to see strength and I was not about to send men out for a pointless war to see it. I just am not the young king that they see strength in anymore.

Orrin, on the left of me, cleared his throat, bringing my attention back to them.

"Sir, you called us this early for what reason?"

"Did something happen when the nobles came in last night?"

"Is the princess-"

Question after question was starting to fly and little time for me to get a word in. I lift my hand and everyone immediately shuts their lips. I let the silence deafen so there was no confusion.

"The princess is fine. First, I want to say thank you to everyone being here. Even you Valin, I know this is one of your few days off." Valin had his arms crossed and was standing at the door. Ready to listen to what I had to say.

"I just want to know if everything is in place." I was nervous and rightfully so, but I would not be doing this tournament if it wasn't for the council members wanting to see the strength in marriage. There was a round of sighs from everyone but Valin. He was the youngest person at this meeting. He earned it after the year of work he put in to get this position.

Valin pushed himself off the wall and placed his hands on the table. The table that held the wooden model of the kingdom. He pointed at and moved a few soldier pieces.

"I have more men posted at these gates. There were a few

posted on these weak points and I was able to take in everyone's profile last night. No one came in that wasn't supposed to and with the extra security it should stay that way."

He gave a smile as he spoke. He seemed so sure of himself and that is what I liked about him. He was confident but not cocky. I gave him a nod.

"Everyone was okay with who is signed up for this?" I looked at my councilmen and I watched as they looked between themselves and there was a nod from them all.

"Then you are dismissed. "

There was a round from everyone saying, 'Yes, your majesty'. Everyone one by one started to filter out of the room but Valin stayed put. He looked like he wanted to say something, but I did not press until I watched the last of the men leave the room.

"Did you have something to say?" I ask as I lean back in my chair. I was so tired from all this.

"I want to throw my name in the tournament." He stood up. He looked like that seventeen-year-old unsure boy again.

"Okay."

"Okay?"

"You have my blessing. But you have to keep your duties. So plan around them. You know the tentative schedule, so make it happen." I found myself stroking my bread as I talked. I could see the relief as his stance slacked to my words.

"Yes, Your Majesty." His smile was evident as he bowed deeply and left the meeting room.

I wait until the door is closed when I pull out the letters from my pocket. The letters had become well worn, but I still held onto them.

Arabella: A new competitor

I was summoned earlier than usual this morning. A private conversation with father was all I was told. I stepped into the washroom and clean up quickly. With the help of the maids, I never really understood why royals couldn't wash themselves. It was ridiculous.

They help me into my long dress, and tied my corset extra tight, making me worry about my ribs breaking.

I sit down as two of the maids argued over whether my hair should be down, curly or up and neat. I rolled my eyes. It was the same argument every day. Eventually they agreed on a half up, half down hairstyle.

There was a knock, and the door slowly opens, revealing my father's guard.

"The king is ready to see you now, princess," he said quickly bowing and walking out.

I sigh, standing up and straightening my dress. My guard on shift when Val isn't around escorts me today. Owen was a big, bulky man with absolutely no conversation whatsoever.

Arabella: A new competitor

He escorts me down the halls and to my father's chambers. I knocked on softly, hearing a quiet "Come in." I open the door bowing to my father and walk in, shutting the door behind me.

"You wanted to see me?" I ask. His face softened as he gesturs to the couch. I sat, and he sat next to me.

"One of our conditions to you agreeing to marry was for me to tell you every information and every change that happens," he comments and I nod my hands feeling slightly sweaty. "Valin has made the decision to join the tournament, as of this morning, and I agreed to his request," Father said. His eyes watching my reaction carefully.

I am surprised. My eyes went wide for a moment, but then I cleared my throat.

"Do you know why he decided to enter this late?" I ask, trying to sound unaffected as possible. Father shook his head no

"I have a few assumptions, but honestly, this is something you will need to ask Valin yourself. This tournament will not be easy Arabella but Valin is a good man. He will treat you right." He says softly, his hand moving to rest on mine.

"I know, father, maybe I will go speak to him. Thank you for letting me know," I say, giving him a soft kiss on his cheek and a bow. I walk out of the door and take a deep breath.

Walking down the long hallways, my brain mixed with different thoughts, with different questions. Owen was close behind me. I arrived at Val's door. I look at Owen.

"I will speak with Valin alone. Please wait outside," I order. He nods, resting his back on the wall and his arms crossed.

I knock on the door softly. There are soft shuffling noises and then the door opens revealing Val wearing a simple tunic and pants. It was a pleasant change to see him in comfortable clothes compared to his guard wear. I smile softly and lift my chin to look up at him.

"Hi, can we talk?" I ask nervously.

There was a moment of pause as he looks between me and Owen. A moment of confusion. He gave me a nod.

"Yes?" He stood there holding the door, still not making a move away. He looks confused.

I bite my lip, feeling a wave of awkwardness wash over me. I look left and to the right down the empty hallways, then back at Val.

"You want to have this conversation out here? Do you not want to invite your princess inside?" I ask, lifting my chin further up, trying to make myself look more assertive but it was very uncomfortable. My neck felt as if it was cramping but I had to keep my confident act going. Otherwise, I would look stupid.

He rubs the back of his neck and steps aside.

"Apologies, Of course. Um, come in."

I grin, feeling victorious. Looking back at Owen and he stands there, staring at me as if I had something unpleasant on my face. I frown and then walk inside, looking at Val's room.

"This is….. nice," I attempted a compliment and turn to face him, intertwining my fingers together in front of me.

He stood a few feet away, and with his hands clasped behind him. He was relaxed, but there was still a stiffness about him.

"You need something?" Always to the point.

I clear my throat; I felt a small amount of uneasiness in my chest. The feeling of something trying to claw its way out of my heart.

"I heard from Father that you have decided to enter the tournament," I state moving closer to him so we were two feet apart. He did not move, but his face was unreadable.

Arabella: A new competitor

"Does that bother you?"

I shake my head no and rest my hand on the back of the lounge chair. It was rough and not soft like the ones in my room. I quickly discarded my hand from it.

"Does it bother me? No, I'm just surprised and wondering why you made this decision." There was a moment of relief that washes over him but back to his soldier self.

"I just wanted to see how I would fair, I guess."

I frown and nod, turning my back to him, walking further into the room to where the window is. I look out at the gardens and sigh.

"Do you understand what you are signing up for? If you win, we will be married and you will be a king. Any freedom you have will be gone. Is that what you want?" I ask.

"I understand. I don't make decisions on impulse."

I turn to face him again, but don't make a move. I contemplate for a moment what I could say to him. To try to understand his actions.

"And do you think you could handle me as your queen?" I question. There was a smile that played on his face.

"I think I have handled you well so far. Wouldn't you think?"

I couldn't help but blush at words, I quickly stood straight and patted my dress.

"I don't know what you are implying, Val."

"Nothing, don't worry about it. Was there anything else?" He starts to walk towards the door but pauses. Waiting for me to say something.

"Do you think you could love me if we married?" I blurt out, but quickly put a hand on my mouth to stop myself from saying anything else. My eyes were wide at my own outburst.

There was a deep sigh. He reached out for the door and

grasps the handle. Before he turns it, and he meets my gaze. There was a softness about them.

"I don't think that will be a problem." He opens the door and steps out. Looking over his shoulder, "I have something to clear up. If that is all, I must leave." He waited.

I felt my heart race for a moment at his words. He was truly a knight. I nod and bow my head at him.

"That is all. I'm glad you chose to enter the tournament," I say, smiling at him and walk out of the door into the hallway.

"See you soon Val" I look to Owen nodding at him to follow as I journey to my room, Owen following closely behind as Val's words repeat in my head. Could he love me? He seemed so sure there was no hesitation. *Could I love him?* I shake my head at my own ridiculous question to myself. Of course I could.

Aerilyn: Make me

I wake the next morning to the servants coming in. They ask me if I wanted to eat breakfast in bed, but I told them no in hopes I would be joining Arabella this morning. They help me into one of my favorite maroon dresses. This one was worn with a corset underneath. That part I did not fancy, but I put up with it. Telling myself that beauty is pain.

My hair was halfway up. I wanted to let my hair flow down to cover my backside. The dress was not terribly deep, but I liked the feeling of my hair touching. They only pulled back some of my side pieces just so my face was left uncovered.

I gave the dress a quick spin before leaving. One of the maids stops me from leaving without my shoes. With a huff, I stick my feet out for them to put them on. I held onto the door frame. I could hear footsteps coming down the hallway. With my newfound balancing act, I lean back to get a look down the hall. It was just that guy from the night before.

"Good morning!" I gave him my best smile. He looks up as if I just interrupted his thoughts.

"Morning." His voice is deep and vibrating within me.

"I'm Aerilyn," I said, trying to keep his attention.

"Yes, I know. Your Grace." My last shoe was now on, and I was leaning my back on the threshold. He made it in front of me, giving a quick nod to the maid and bowing to me.

"Are you going to tell me your name?" I called after him as he started down the stairs from my room.

"Valin," He yells back but did not turn around.

The name sounded like it was familiar, but I just shrugged it off. I walked down the hall and down the other set of stairs so I could make it to the dining room.

Walking in and see the dining room was almost vacant. I saw my father talking to someone and tried to turn to leave before he found me. As I turn, I hear him clear his throat. I had half a mind to pretend I did not hear him. He would find me if he wanted me, so I decided to rip it off like a bandage.

"Father!" I said, a little too happy. He did not seem bothered by it. The gentleman sitting next to him looks to be maybe a few years older than I. He had stood as I walk into the room. He had blonde hair that was cut short. His face looks cleanly shaved, which might make him look younger than he was.

I walk toward him and my father. Standing in front of this man, I saw that he was the same height I was. It was hard to find men taller than I, like Valin. I feel a quick flash of warmth cross my face as the gentleman takes my hand to place a kiss. I am sure he thinks it was for him and I would never say out loud what I was thinking about.

"Pleasure to meet you, Aerilyn. I'm Sir Keiran. I have heard a lot from your father, and I hope to spend some time with you while you are here." He had let my hand go and pulled a chair out for me. I hesitate for a moment.

Aerilyn: Make me

If I sit, I would be stuck in conversation for who knows how long. I had no interest in knowing more about this man, but I could not anger him or my father. So I smile sweetly.

"I have already eaten, but I thank you for your thought. I would love to get to know you more, but I have someone to meet. Talks with ladies are in need at this moment." There was a look of sadness on his face, but he did not argue with me.

"I look forward to seeing you soon, then." I left before my father could say a thing about this. He looks disappointed, and he was not one to keep his opinions to himself.

I had no idea where Arabella was, but I did not want to ask and look desperate. It wasn't like she left the grounds often, according to the letters she sent me. I walk to the gardens.

Their garden hedges looked like something from a fairytale book. Shaped and trimmed in various whimsical things. I make my way to the maze. It was so pretty, with various flowers growing in vines over the maze walls.

Walking through the maze, I thought I heard someone just up head. I followed the twists and turns. Catching glimpses of someone just before they turned out of sight again. I could not make out if it was a male or female.

I gather some of my skirts of my dress and quicken my steps. I yell out Arabella's name. It felt like a chase game from when we were kids.

I turn the corner and run straight into someone. My head smacks their back. I would have fallen if it wasn't for them grabbing me. Rubbing my nose and look up at this person. I had to blink a few times, as I could not believe who I was seeing.

Valin had caught me by my waist, and his other hand had a hold of my elbow. He helps me steady on my feet and looks bewildered. Probably just as much as I was.

"Oh, I-" he cut me off, bringing his finger over his lips. Telling me to be quiet. He kept his hands on me and looked around us. I clear my throat softly as I was becoming increasingly aware of our placement. My back pressed along one of the hedges. His leg bent into my dress. His hands are still on me. We were so close I thought I could hear his heart beating in my ears, but I wondered if it was my own pulse rushing. I tighten my grip on his shirt.

"Tell me what you are looking for, at least?" I keep my tone very low. I barely could hear them over the sounds of pounding hearts.

There was a small tightness around my waist. Then he looks down at me. I felt as if I could not breathe as he peered down at me with his green eyes. I thought as if it held the deep of the woods inside of them.

"I thought I saw someone." He moves away from me, and I felt the instant cold of his absence. "What are you doing out here, anyway?" I felt as if he was accusing me of something. Like I was a child caught with their hand in the cookie jar.

"I was looking for the princess."

"She isn't here. You should leave." I felt brushed off, foolish. I turn and realize I have no idea how to get out. Before I turn around, I hear him sigh.

"You don't know how to get out, do you?" Before I could reply, he gets in front of me and leads me out. I had a hard time keeping up, but I managed.

Once we were out of the maze, I start to smooth out my dress. I look up to tell him thank you, but he was already walking away. I shake off my thoughts and make my way back inside the palace.

Arabella: Confessions of a Princess

Sitting on the edge of the bed, I wait for her arrival. Valin told me he caught her getting lost in the maze today while he was securing the grounds. Grinning at the image of her sense of direction failing her. I told Valin to summon her here so we could spend some time together and yet my heart was beating nervously. I shared many letters with her in the time we were apart and didn't receive anything back. Maybe she was still dealing with her father; he was always so hot headed with her and when we were younger, I would always remember her complaining about his strictness or maybe she was over me and I prayed that it wasn't the case.

There was a knock on the door.

"Come in" I shout and Valin opens the door. I straighten my back quickly.

"Princess, Aerilyn is here to see you" I glare at him, we have talked about the princess talk but every time he keeps saying princess. Aerilyn pushes past Valin. She was holding a bottle of wine and two glasses with it.

"No need to announce my presence Valin, she knows who I am." Aerilyn grins, walking over to me and giving me the biggest hug. I grin and hug her back. Looking over her shoulder at Valin, I nod to him.

"We are fine alone Valin please wait outside" I say and he bows shutting the door without any other conversation from him. I roll my eyes one of these days I'll get him out of his shell.

"Formal as ever," Aerilyn muses looking back to me.

"Tell me about it," I grumble back and sit on the bed. Aerilyn following close behind. "I keep telling him to call me Arabella when no one else is around but he chooses not to follow that order."

Once we were sat on the bed she pops open the wine with ease and I look at her with awe at how easy it was, she shrugged as if it were nothing and poured a glass for me giving it to me and pouring one for herself.

"So the summon you gave sounded serious. Is everything okay?" She asks, taking a sip of her wine.

"Yes, everything is fine, well I think it's fine. The tournament is coming up and things got interesting," I say and take a big gulp of wine and then scrunch my nose up at it with how strong it was. Internally, I make a note to take smaller sips.

"Oh?" she says, her face looking curious now. I clear my throat and scratch the back of my neck. I lean forward towards her and lower my voice in case Val could hear us.

"Valin has decided to be a competitor in the tournament." My finger goes on my lip as if to motion for her to be quiet, too.

"Valin? Tall, broody all business, Valin? Why?"

"Yes, the Valin that is outside my door Valin. I tried asking him but his answer was… inexplicit, he wouldn't give me a proper answer to me asking him why," I say.

"Maybe he is embarrassed?"

"Embarrassed? We are talking about Valin here, strong, independent Valin. I don't know. I've been trying to get an answer from him, but he won't tell me. I wonder if Father is forcing him to join," I sigh.

"I can find out if you want."

"Find out? How?" I ask her nervously.

"I am pretty good at getting information.."

"Please don't do something that will get you into trouble Aerilyn, I'm already worrying over this more than I thought I would be," I finish the glass of wine and felt the alcohol go straight to my head, I really should have ate before drinking this wine.

Aerilyn took my empty glass from me and leaned in.

"Me in trouble? I will be fine." I frown and shake my head.

"You're Aerilyn, and trouble is your middle name. This whole situation is making me nervous." I rub my forehead.

After setting our cups down, she got closer to me. The back of her hand ran over my forehead and then gently follows down my cheek. The touch of her hand felt like it was everywhere. How could her touch make me feel so alive?

"I will be fine. Just try to relax." I dramatically fall back onto the bed and look up at the ceiling.

"I guess I'll have to find a way to get you out of the dungeons if all goes wrong," I joke, a smile playing on my lips. "Maybe a joust with the guards on shift or a simple game of cards," I grin.

The bed shift as she climbs and lays down next time me. I felt her gently take my hand in hers and just curls up next to me.

"You be my savior? I think I might like that."

I smile and lie on my side, looking at her. I remember all the feelings I felt in the past brewing back up, but I swallow it back down.

"One day, when I become queen, I will make it my royal decree that you are to marry whoever you wish. Because you are a rare jewel Aerilyn"

There was a sad smile and a soft kiss on my knuckles.

"That is, if I wanted to marry." She said and got back up. "I think I better go to bed or I might fall asleep here."

I laugh and sit up, too. I gave her a soft kiss on her cheek as I stand with her.

"Yes, I should probably change for bed, have a good night Aerilyn" I grin and take off the jewelry in my ears. There was a pause. I thought she would say something, but she left. Leaving the empty bottle and glasses.

Valin: That Damned Temptress

It was my last day off, and every day it has been something between the princess and the duchess. I felt as though the two of them had made it their mission to torment me. I feel as though I can no longer look at the princess because she looks up at me like I am about to make her dreams come true. When in truth I want nothing more than to find a close dark corner and have my way with her. That was far from the innocence she looks up at me with.

Then there is Aerilyn. If biting her lip was a religion, she did so faithfully. There was always a playfulness about her. The line of teasing, walking on a tightrope, and falling was the promise of a fiery end. I'm pretty sure if I advance on her, I could have my way with her. But did I? I did, but I shouldn't. I just had to keep reminding myself that she would be leaving soon. Plus, I am sure most of it was a flirtatious front, as she looks as if she desired the princess.

I walked into the library so I would have some peace. Grabbing a few books to poke around. I had no intention of getting sucked into anything, just want the solitude. There were many empty tables. I chose one at random that looks to be in the dark. I corner myself and prop my feet up as I open the book.

I was undisturbed for a good while. Hell, I probably would have started to doze. A nice nap on a nice day off, but I heard the shuffle of feet coming towards me. I close my book and look at who is approaching.

Aerilyn with a wine chalice in hand. The sway of her hips as she walks towards me. The look of trouble. She must have been wearing a corset underneath today. The purple dress clung to her small waist as the rest of the skirt was filled and touching the floor. Her dress barely contained her breasts. I found myself hoping to see more, even if it was by accident. I forced my eyes away and looks up at her smiling red lips.

"Busy, Valin?" She plays my name on her tongue. Like she was testing how it sound it sounded out loud. Just a bit low in tone and it would sound like a moan of my name. I curse my thoughts as I feel the tight desire of wanting to hear her say my name just like that.

"No, why?" Her eyes twinkled with mischievousness.

"No reason. I figured we could talk."

"What now, Aerilyn?"

"Now? I have never tried to talk to you. I have been here a few days, and I heard you were this big bad knight that stays with the princess always, but I never see you there. I wanted to see if it was a rumor." She pushes my feet off the chair I had them lying in. Sitting in that chair and forcing me to sit up some.

"I had a few days off."

"You looked busy. Aren't you supposed to have fun on your

days off or do you just enjoy stalking the princess?"

"Stalking? You are funny. Funnier than you used to be." My words trailed off, and I realized what I said when I saw her surprise.

"Used to be? What do you mean? Have we met?" She had crossed her legs, and she sat down, but now she was leaning over them. Her elbow resting on her knee. I could see the brush of her breast on her arm with every breath she exhaled.

"I don't know what I mean. Poor choice of words, I suppose." She narrowed her eyes at me.

"I heard you threw your name in the tournament. Do you plan to win?"

"Doesn't hurt to try."

"Hm, do you have a plan for if you fail?" She took a sip of her wine. She leans closer, and I was not sure how that was possible.

"I will go back to doing what I was doing."

"Is that what you want?" She asks me and only one other person has asked me that.

"I think."

"You know, I am supposed to look for someone to court while everyone is gathered in one place. I can't seem to find anyone. Or maybe someone has caught my eye." She looks like she was drinking me in. Running her finger over her lower lip. I thought that she might have been talking about the princess, but now I was not so sure. I dare not ask. She stands, setting her cup on the table next to my book. She brushes her fingertips over my hand before she turns and walks away.

If I were a different person, I would have followed her. I would have found the nearest room to steal a moment with her. To take her open invitation. She played the bored, neglected noble's wife, looking for fun. I stared at that damn glass, trying to chase the thoughts of the lewd face she would make if I had just followed her.

Arabella: Meeting the competition

I sit at my vanity, staring at my reflection. The maids were poking and prodding me with makeup brushes. One was curling my hair, though I do wonder if she was to leave me with any hair after she was finished with how rough she was pulling.

My eyes close to allow the maids to add color to my eyes. Once I open them and look at the finished result, I frown at how different I look. This wasn't me. The maids all gave small claps at their finished work, gushing at how beautiful I looked, but deep inside I felt they just added a mask to my face, to hide the real me.

I step into the dress that the maids had prepared. It was a beautiful pink dress with gold specs around it. I brace my hands on the bottom rail of the bed, the maid ties my corset tightly and I can feel the material pushing up my chest, I roll my eyes at the thought of men only being appeased by how big my assets were rather than how I am personally.

I walk out of the room and nod to Owen. Val has taken

a couple of days away from work, and I have had Owen watch over me more often. I missed Val; I missed his blunt conversations. Miss the way his eyes would look over my body when he thought I wasn't looking. I bite my lip at this thought as we walked to the empty lounge room.

We walk inside, and I sit down in the comfortable chair. The table in front of me had a beautiful, flowery tea set. One of the butlers in the room pours me a cup and handed it to me and bows. I smile, nodding my head at him in thanks and sip it. The tea was hot but didn't burn my lips. It was a tasty jasmine today that made my taste buds tingle.

The door opens, and I placed the cup of tea back onto the table and stood up, facing the man who had walked in. He was tall and slim; wearing what looked to be very expensive linen and a beige coat. He smiles softly at me. His face was soft and young, probably in his early twenties.

"Your highness" he says bowing to me and holds my hand and kisses the back of it softly. I blush and smile back at him.

"It is lovely to meet you, Sir?"

"Oh, how rude of me, my name is Sir Gregory, I do have a gift for you," he says nodding to his guard and a giant bouquet appear from behind the guard's back. It was a beautiful bunch full of roses and lilies, not my favorite flowers, but I wouldn't say this to him. I just smile, nodding to one of the butlers in the room to take the flowers off him.

"How kind of you, thank you very much, please sit," I say, motioning him to the chairs. I sat on one side where he sat on the other. The butlers offered him tea as well, which he accepted, not thanking them once he receives it. I frown but brushed it off. Maybe he is distracted.

I looked up into his eyes to start asking a question, but I

Arabella: Meeting the competition

noticed his eyes were staring at my breasts. Looking down at them too, they were bigger thanks to the corset I was wearing, but they weren't out bare to this man. I frown and cleared my throat.

"So, what are your plans if you are to win the tournament? Becoming a king is a tough role to fill"

He finally looks up and smiles at me.

"Well, princess, as king, I will rule the country, as is my job. I would like for you to bear as many heirs as possible, so that will keep you busy. Every woman desires to be a mother, am I wrong?" He asks, moving the cup to his lips and taking a sip.

I look at him in shock. I wasn't expecting that response from him.

"Bare many heirs? Like, how many are you thinking?"

"Oh, I don't know, ten? Fifteen maybe, we will have plenty of time once we are married," he muses, and I felt sick.

The rest of our conversation ends up being about how he would rule the kingdom. He doesn't believe that his queen needs to be out greeting the country, his wife should always be kept safe behind castle walls. To him my job in the married is keep giving him children and busy myself with them all day every day.

A servant walked in telling me time was up and I have never been so thankful to hear it. We both stand up.

"It was a pleasure meeting you, princess. I look forward to our long lives together." He grins, kissing my hand again, and I try my best to give him a smile back.

"I will see you at the tournament Sir Gregory."

The moment the door closes behind him, I sigh with relief that he was finally gone. The whole time we talked he wouldn't stop staring at my chest. I think half of his conversations he was talking to them; I shiver and shake my head.

"Princess, the next contender is here," the butler announces. I nod and stand up, waiting for the door to open.

Once the door opens, I see a man wearing relatively smart clothes, however I frown once I take him fully in. He had to at least be in his seventies.

I bow to him, and he grins, bowing his head towards me. I stand up straight, keeping my hands clasped in front of me.

"Princess Arabella it is lovely to meet you I'm Philip and I bring you a special gift from my home" he says and grabs a covered basket from his guard and holds it out to me I slowly grab the blanket to pull it up so I could see what's inside and to my shock was a basket full of rats, once the blanket is lifted some of them crawl onto my arm and that was when I lost it, I scream and jump away from the basket. Owen and two other guards ran into the room. Owen pushing me behind him, looking around for danger. He calms down when he sees rats running around the floor. Butlers were running around trying to catch all of them. Once they had all been caught, they took them out of the room, allowing me to calm down. The whole time this was happening, he had been laughing, finding this amusing.

We sat down, and name was offered tea which he politely refused.

"So tell me about yourself," I say, taking a sip of the tea.

"Well, I was married once but my late wife passed away from by influenza, so now I enjoy chess to keep the old brain going and keeping watch over the animals we have. I will have to show you someday princess"

I nod and listen to his story, but my brain couldn't stop wondering why my father allowed a man into this tournament that was this old.

The day goes on and I meet each and every competitor. I was praying each time that I would not get anymore animal gifts from any of them. One of the men was a sweet-looking man that honestly I could see potential in, but to rule a kingdom? Far from it. He kept telling me silly jokes and acting like he was a toddler. The bear he had given me was sweet, though the last thing I needed was stuffed animals.

Another man came in and he acted as if he was forced to be there. There was no gift, though that may have been a blessing in disguise at this point with how awful today has gone. The man had given me one-word answers for everything I would ask or mention and honestly, talking to a brick wall sounded more entertaining than that was.

The next man that came in had given me a chicken, though much to my surprise, he didn't have this animal covered. I saw it the moment he came into the room. This Lord had talked and talked. I didn't get a word in. He was so busy talking about himself that I lost interest after minutes of him being in the room.

The next competitor who came saw me and rolled his eyes as if my appearance was appalling to him. He sat there and stared at my body as if he was sizing up my body and judging what he was seeing. The gift he had given was a rose, which would have been sweet. However, the rose was black and looked as if it was plucked days ago.

Another man walked in. My head at this point was slightly painful, but I smile at him as he nods and takes my hand. We sit down and I learn his name is Keiran.

"So I hear you're good friends with the duchess?" He asks and I frown, finding it an odd thing to talk about during one of these meetings, but I will entertain him.

"Aerilyn? Oh yes, we have been friends since I can remember. Do you know of her?"

"Only in passing, I suppose, tell me, is she a fan of flowers just like you princess?" he asks, looking around at the large range of flowers in the room that I had collected from the gentlemen today.

"Oh, I mean she would appreciate the thought, of course, but she prefers the taste of fine wine," I explain. He was asking a lot about Aerilyn, I look down and see both of my fists were clenched tight into fists. I relax them and look up and saw Keiran was staring at me, waiting for an answer. "Oh my apologies, what was it you said?" I ask.

"I said my time is up, princess. I must be off. I have a meeting with a duke to get to," I nod and stand up. He bows and quickly leaves the room. What a strange man he was.

I sigh, feeling hope is lost. None of these men screamed king or husband to me. I felt sick to my stomach at the thought of this being my life, spending all my days with any of these men.

There was a knock at the door, and I slowly stood up, waiting for it to open. My heart was racing erratically and when it opens, I felt like everything had stilled, my heart skipped and my mouth went dry, it was Valin. He was wearing a cream-colored shirt that had a layer of frills. His shirt was neatly tucked into a pair of black pants. He walked in holding a variety of flowers that looked like it was from the field. My heart fluttered at the thought of him going around the gardens personally, picking each flower.

I clear my throat and quickly wiped my bottom lip with the back of my hand, wiping away any drool that may have fallen. I smile up at him and bow slightly.

Arabella: Meeting the competition

"It's nice to finally see you after a couple of days Sir Valin" He hands over the flowers. The servant comes up and takes them for me.

"For you, and did you miss me?"

I grin and shrug, moving to sit on the chair I pat the space next to me.

"Miss you? Of course, Owen hasn't been too talkative with me," I joke.

"Not that I have much to say, either. I will be honest, I did not think this far ahead. What happens now? I heard there were questions, but I feel like I know everything there is to know."

He moves to sit next to me and I lean on my side, looking at him.

"Well, the first man who came in talked about me baring as many heirs as possible and the second man I'm pretty sure he may die of old age before the tournament starts so anything is a plus, however we don't have to talk we can just drink tea and then end our private time if that is to your liking," I say and pass him a cup of tea.

He takes the cup, and it looked like it was foreign for him to even touch it. He took a drink though, but set the cup back on the table.

"Thank you, but I think I will pass on the tea. Is there anything you want to know? I think you grilled me pretty hard, but I won't shy away from more questions."

I lean back in my chair; the corset digging uncomfortably into my ribs; I ponder something to ask.

"What made you want to become a guard, Val?"

"Ambitious. Why does anyone want anything that makes them better?"

I rest my chin on my hand, staring at him intently, trying to figure out how to get him to open up to me.

"A question answered with a question, how Val of you" I smirk at my joke. I move my hand to his and place it against his, his hand being much bigger than mine.

"You have big hands, very important to have as a guard. You have strong muscles also important to have as a guard, so you have the physical attributes to be one, but do you have the mentality of a guard?" I ask, stroking my finger up and down his biceps.

There was a physical tension at the touch. I watch as he moves uncomfortably trying not to offend me. But he didn't move away from my touch completely.

"I did answer the question but rebuttal with a question. Isn't that how you keep a conversation going? As for mentality, I think I have made it this far. I don't think I am one to brag about those things."

"Well, if both of them are good, as you say, then you are a good candidate to become my husband. I think I only have one question to ask. Have you ever been with another woman, Val? Are you experienced with a female's body?" I ask pushing my chest to him, it felt so unnatural but I had read it in a book that sometimes women do it and it made them attractive to a man, but now that I was doing it I regretted the action, wondering if this made me look stupid or desperate, but I didn't stop.

There was a moment when he seemed to drink me in. He dare to look at what was not his yet but so seamlessly offered in a moment. Just to look, as there would not be time to explore. His eyes trailed over me and up to my face. Time seemed to have stopped. His expression was soft, and he looked like a prince, like my prince. I couldn't stop the blush on my

Arabella: Meeting the competition

face or my burning skin against his. In this moment, Val was everything I wanted and more.

He took my hand in his, holding my gaze, and placed a soft kiss. There was a shuffle of feet and the doors opened, indicating the time was up.

"I think my time is up, princess."

Mentally I curse whoever opened the doors, but I look at Val and stand up slowly and bow my head.

"Thank you for your time, Sir Val. I look forward to seeing you in the tournament," I say in a professional tone, as if that moment between us didn't happen. There was a smile that plays on his lips.

"Of course," he said as he left.

I watch him leave. The touch of his lips on my hand was tingling. My legs feel like jelly, so I sit down on the chair to compose myself. The look in his eyes made me feel emotions that I had never felt before. My heart almost hurt with the need of how much I wanted this man more than romantically. I wanted him physically, too.

Once composed, Owen escorted me to my room, and I was helped into a nightgown by my lady-in-waiting and I lay in bed almost wishing Val was here. I wondered if he would come if I asked but then I remembered how much of a gentleman he was, I sigh and close my eyes drifting off into a deep slumber.

Aerilyn: That inevitable Day

My days have been spent running from my father's suitors. I knew it was going to make him mad, but how he found so many that were not joining the fight for the princess's hand, I have no idea. I thought I would have had some peace from the constant cornering my father and picks did.

They were not bad men, but I felt no desire for them. I wanted someone to stir the dance of fires within me. I wanted to not feel like another jewelry piece that would be forgotten until it was convenient for them. Either way, I was not escaping this day.

I was awoken by the banging on my door. I barely had time to sit up in bed when my father just barged in. Pulling my covers up, knowing the nightgown I wore did little to cover.

It was unlike him to just come see me, but then again, this was the first time he wanted me to do something. I have been so blatantly defiant.

He storms into my room and starts to pace the floor. His

Aerilyn: That Inevitable Day

face was red and swollen. There were dark circles under his eyes. He was mad and seemed to not have slept last night. I find myself involuntarily tense. He was never one to hit, but it was rare to see him this mad, either.

"Do you realize the damage you are doing?" I hold my tongue. Nothing I could say would help the situation. I simply stay where I am and just let him yell it out.

"Pfft! Of course, you don't! Insolent girl. I don't know how to put this to make you understand." He had stopped pacing and raised his hand to add more, but held his tongue a few times.

"You will get dressed. You will look your best. You will meet Sir Keiran in mid-morning. He wants to court you. Why, I don't understand, but this will happen. You will be attending the first festive day with him. There will be no excuses for leaving. Understand?" He stayed even after I had nodded. I knew he was waiting to hear me say the words.

"Yes, I understand." After I finally respond, He stormed back out and slammed the door so hard it bounced back open. I had fought back the dread and sorrow. I was not one to dwell on self-pity, but some days were harder than others.

I finally drag my feet to the floor and put a robe over my shoulders. There was a soft knock at the door that had me spinning around. I thought maybe my Father was not finished yet. As I turn, I cross my robe to cover myself again.

"The door was open, and I thought I heard yelling. Is everything okay?" Valin was standing there in his full uniform. He must be getting ready to be on duty. I could feel the threat of the tears starting to spill. I bite my lower lip to distract myself.

"I am fine." For a moment I thought he might leave, but he

turns again to walk into the room. He left the door open but closed the space between us.

"You don't have to tell me what is going on, but it is okay not to be fine." I felt my heart start to shatter. I wanted to wrap my arms around him and him to hold me. To hold on so tight that it allowed me to have a moment to just fall apart because he was there holding me back together.

But I stay where I am and look away from his gentle eyes. I hear him move and was prepared for him to leave, but he didn't. He reaches up, dragging his thumb across my cheek. The palm of his hand easily cups my face.

There is a moment when he drags his thumb along my lip. His dark, inquisitive look as his thumb gently pulls my lower lip down. A moment of weakness comes over me as I start to stand on my toes to meet his lips. I just want a distraction. Something to force me out of my head. To forget all the negative thoughts of how much of a failure I am.

The maids that had helped me every morning start to enter. The sounds of their entry had Valin, and I both freeze. Frozen and oh so close. Valin clears his throat and takes a step back.

"Aerilyn," He says my name as a goodbye as he bows and left me standing in my room. The cold breeze reminding me to close my robes back up. The head maid closes the door and says nothing about what had almost happened.

I appreciate there was no gossip about it. They help me dress in a deep blue dress. Underneath, they tried to put on a full corset, but I opted for the one that did not squeeze my ribs too much. It still lifted my breast nicely, but breathing was an option.

I assured the head maid that I did not plan on eating, so I would not have to worry about bloating. Once they help me in my laced boots, I insisted that my hair be half down. If I was to play the good daughter, I wanted to have my hair down. It was the nicest thing about me. My long chestnut hair waved down to my waist and made me feel gorgeous.

* * *

There were tents and people everywhere.

I clasp my hands together and wait by the fountain. I try to not look like I was desperate, but I was starting to second-guess this meeting. In fact, if I would be doing it. I guess it would be nice to have someone to walk and talk with.

I see Sir Keiran walking towards me. He wasn't in his normal fashion. He looks to be dressed for participation in the tournament today. I hold my tongue, but it wasn't long before he was in front of me and I let the words fly.

"Sir Keiran, what are you dressed in today?" I tried to keep my tone sweet, but I could taste the sour on my tongue. He gave a curt bow.

"It's for today. I was going to tell you that I had joined, but I have not been able to find you as of late." We start to walk. Where to I did not know.

"Yes, I did not know you fancied the princess."

"Well, to be honest, who doesn't? But I am not doing it for her."

"But that is the whole point of playing these dangerous games."

"For most, yes. I think I just wanted to see how I fair." I felt silly for even bringing it up now.

"I see."

"Do you? I hope I do see you cheering me on. I was hoping

to have your favor."

"You were hoping for mine?" I was completely taken back. I was not used to this. I tried to avoid situations like this.

"Yes, I heard you would be sitting next to the princess. By heard I wanted to make sure you were not by yourself while I was occupied."

"You thought of me?"

"Of course, I think about you a lot as of late." I should have felt butterflies. Instead of feeling flattered, I felt the guilt of my own actions. I thought of him not at all. I had spent all this time chasing the odd desire for Valin and begging the princess to look at me. Torn between two people that have no desire for me while he was here. Thought of me so much that he did not want me to be alone.

"Thank you," I could only bring myself to say. I took his arm as we walked. We spent the remainder in small talk and looking at all the vendors that took an opportunity to set up. Maybe it was time to give it all up.

Arabella: When darkness comes

Everything was dark, almost as if I was floating in a black room which I had no control over. I wonder if this was some form of sleep paralysis, but something felt off.

The darkness fades, and then there was a light far in the distance. I walk slowly towards it. Squeezing my eyes tightly shut as I walk into the sun. I look around and was in the town. It looks run down. People who were in the houses quickly shut their windows and shut the curtains as I walk by.

I felt like I knew this place, a place I love here. There was a butterfly which was flying in front of my face. I step back, but it kept fluttering its wings and then flew away. When I didn't move, it came back and fluttered in my face again. I felt in my gut that I need to follow it.

As it flew away again, I slowly ascend towards it. My dream felt so real, like I was really here.

I follow the butterfly all the way over to an open field. There were wildflowers everywhere. It was gorgeous. It also looked as if I had been here before, but I knew that was ridiculous.

I walk further into the field and frown at seeing a man holding a bleeding woman. She was dead. The man's body was shaking as if he was letting out a quiet sob. My heart ached for him. I walk closer towards these two people. I need to see if I could offer him any help. That was until I froze seeing the woman's appearance. She looks exactly like me. I was so shocked that I couldn't move.

"I will find you again," I hear the man say, and I frown. He didn't sound like he had been crying. Just as that thought came into my head, he lays my body, her body, onto the ground and stood up. He turns to face me, but the hood obscures his face. I could only see his chin.

Be wary of those with hearts of gold. The greed of others will take them to hoard.

My whole body went numb. I was in shock. The man's chin didn't move, so the words didn't come from his mouth, but it was definitely his voice. I gulp, anxiously wondering what he was talking about. I look to where he was standing, and he was gone, as if he had never been there. That was until I felt somebody behind me and I tense, feeling his breath behind my ear.

"We will meet again soon," he whispers.

I sit up in bed quickly and look around the room. I gasp for breath at how realistic the dream felt. My heart races erratically. I wipe the sweat off my forehead and shakily get out of the bed. I needed to get some air.

As I change into a simple dress that flowed to my ankles,

Arabella: When darkness comes

I walk out of the door. Owen stood up still and looks at me questioningly.

"Couldn't sleep." I smile sheepishly.

He nods and I slowly walk down the hall, Owen close by.

I walked for a few minutes just wondering around, trying to clear my mind when I hear quiet mutters in the hall around the corner. I frown and get close but was still out of sight; I peer and see two maids. Pulling back before they can see me. I knew eavesdropping was wrong, but the curiosity won over my sense of self.

"Did you hear? One of the hand maids said she saw duchess Aerilyn and Sir Valin being very, very close. She said she swore she thinks they kissed," one maid said. I frown at hearing what they were saying about Aerilyn and Val. I felt a small amount of jealousy in my chest and I hated myself for that.

"Well, at least he's going for the duchess. What kind of life would he have with a pampered princess who stays locked up in a castle all day, every day," the other maid says and they both laugh.

I feel a tear trickle down my cheek hearing their words. Maybe they both would be better without me, better together.

I jump when I feel a hand on my shoulder. I turn my head to see Owen's hand. His face shows worry and I smile at him, softly turning back to face forward and wipe the tear from my cheek. I turn my body and start walking back to my room.

"I'll be fine, Owen, thank you," I say, walking into my room and shutting the door behind me.

I sit at the vanity and grab my favorite book.

For the rest of the night, I didn't sleep. I didn't dare think of sleeping in fear of having another nightmare like the last.

There was a knock at the door. I sit up and put my book

down on the table.

"Come in" I shout and in walks my hand maid. Behind her followed a few others holding different dresses and jewels. She walks over to me and gasps as if she's seen a ghost. My heart starts to race and I look around the room.

"What?" I ask and she holds my chin tightly in-between her fingers and I wince at the force.

"I tell you every time, Princess! You need to have extra sleep when there are big events on. The tournament is today and you will be greeting your future husband! You are going to need a lot of makeups today," she exclaims at me and then sighs.

The next three hours go by quickly. I felt like I zoned out the whole time they were doing my makeup, hair and putting me in my dress. I needed to snap out of all of this.

Food is brought in, it was porridge and fruit as my Maid would say 'to give you substance Princess' I roll my eyes and nibble at it but my stomach was in knots, mostly from the nerves of the trial some from seeing both Aerilyn and Valin. I don't hate them, and I don't blame them. But the feeling of jealousy never went away. I felt jealous because my heart belonged to them both and deep inside, I knew it was wrong.

The door opens, shaking me out of my thoughts. I look up and see Owen.

"Is it time to go?" I ask, and he nods. I stand and twirl in front of him. "How do I look?" I ask, and he just stares at me. Still no words. "I agree, blue isn't my color, but it will have to do. Thank you for the honesty Owen." I smile and walk out of the room to the tournament.

Arabella: These feelings

I pace around the room my finger in my mouth nervously nibbling the nails, the voice of my maid scolding my unladylike actions in my head brought me to a stop, I quickly remove my finger from my mouth and wipe it on my dress.

Looking at the time I frown, Aerilyn wasn't here with wine like normal, in fact come to think of it she hasn't been here for a couple days. I'll have to scold her about that tomorrow.

My brain moved to thoughts of Val, I was so use to him being around everyday now with him doing the tournament I felt like I have barely spoken to him. I sigh sadly, I miss him. He looked good at the tournament but definitely took some hits, *did he see a medic?* I wonder to myself.

Immediately after this thought I made the decision that I needed to see that he was okay. I didn't change into a dress, I stay in my nightgown, smirking to myself.

"Aerilyn's rebellion is rubbing off on me" I say out loud knowing that if I were caught out of my room wearing a nightgown then the maids would have a fit.

I walk out of my door, Owen was in his usual space standing there. He turns to look at me, his eyebrow raised questioningly.

"Don't worry about it, we are going to see how Valin is fairing after the first day" I grin and start walking towards Valin's room.

The journey was quiet, there were no maids or guards in any of the hallways, they must be preparing for the next day of the tournament, Owen kept pace with me occasionally looking around to see if anyone spots us.

I knock on Valin's door and wait for few minutes before I frown, I wonder if he was sleeping already. I knock again and wait, no answer. I check the door handle and see that the door was unlocked.

I look back at Owen and place my finger on my lips.

"Don't tell anyone I'm just making sure he's okay." I say and he looks at me as if I had two heads, I grin and open his door.

The room was dark, but not so dark I couldn't see. I look around the room, it was clean and untouched. I frown confused, did he not return after the fight. I spot one of his jackets on the back of the chair. I pick it up and move it to my nose, I smell the coat and it smelt of him. I hug the coat to my chest tightly imagining it was him and that he was holding me again. Which was until I felt eyes on the back of me as if they were glaring at me, I turn around.

Owen stood at the doorway his hands on his hips and looking at me with judgemental eyes. I quickly throw the jacket back onto the couch and walk back to the door, his stare was still intense on me.

"Owen I'm going to have to ask you to tone the judgement down" I say and he rolls his eyes.

Arabella: These feelings

I sigh and put my hands on my hips wondering where he was.

I guess I could go and look for Aerilyn since she's been missing recently and see what's going on with her, I miss her too I hope I haven't said anything to upset her. The thought of that made my stomach drop. Maybe I shouldn't see her if she is mad at me but even as this thought came into my head my legs had already walking towards her room.

I walk through the halls towards Aerilyn's room feeling defeated. I really wished to see Val tonight just to make sure that he was okay, and to give him an out if it was too much but I knew he would never take it. The man was so stubborn sometimes.

I get to Aerilyn's door and lifted my hand up to knock but frown when I see that the door was ajar slightly, *this woman had no sense of self preservation*, I shake my head slowly popping my head through the door. The fire was creating a glow of light and there on the table was a wine bottle that looked to be missing some of its contents, two wine glasses on the table one stained with the wine that was once there and the other half full. I raise my eyebrows surprise, *she had a guest over?* I wondered.

I look over towards the couch by the table, there entangled was two bodies, one was unmistakably Aerilyn. She hadn't changed the dress. I look up to the faces and froze when I see Aerilyn and Val kissing.

Their tongues explored each others, Vals hand was on Aerilyn's waist roughly pulling her against him, so close.

Aerilyn's bottom half of her body looked as if it was rubbing against Vals body, his moan fills the room. Aerilyn's hands move up to remove his shirt, his bare skin was bruised but other then bruises he lookes like it was fine. Her hands rubbing up and down his body as if she was enjoying the feel of his abs.

Val pulls away slightly, he stares at her with so much emotion that I had never seen from him.

"Gods, I need you so bad." he says and moves his face into her neck kissing her there too, causing her to moan loudly. My face blushes at the scene in front of me, I wanted to move but I felt frozen to that spot.

"Then have me," Aerilyn says moving her hand to Val's cheek bringing him back up to kiss her again.

There was heat radiating from my skin so much I thought I could see steam, or maybe it was the steam coming from the two people in front of me about to make love. The thought of that was enough to knock me out of being frozen, I quickly but quietly pull my head out of the room and shut the door.

I turn and look at Owen.

"Stop being so loud." I whisper causing him to face palm. I quickly move down the hallways and to my room opening the door and quickly shutting it behind me.

My breathing felt heavy, I was almost a witness to an erotica. My body was still so hot which I could probably cook an egg on my skin and it would be sizzling in seconds. I waft my face with my hand hoping to cool me down but it didn't. I move to my bed and sit on it thinking about what I had just seen. My heart was racing and the heat between my legs was unbearable.

I lay in the bed staring at the ceiling. I should really get some sleep I hadn't slept a whole lot last night. I close my eyes and pray that sleep takes me quickly.

Pictures of Aerilyn and Val were playing behind my closed eyelids, even though they were closed I felt like I could see that moment again. The way he kissed her, how he dominated

Arabella: These feelings

every inch of her mouth, how she thrusts her front to his. I open my eyes and gulp, my body has this feeling of need, a need I have never felt before.

I moved my hand to the hem of my dress lifting it up slowly, my fingertips trailing along my skin slowly, my breathing labor.

I slowly took the nightgown off and move it to the side of the bed. I remove my bra to rest on top of my nightgown, I lay back onto the soft pillows behind me prepping me up slightly.

I bite my lower lip and move my hands down to my breast and I move circles around my nipple feeling how hard they were, I bit my lip and close my eyes. I kept circling my nipple and I imagined it was Val's hand rubbing me.

"How long have these been needing attention?" I hear his voice in my head, I picture his tongue sucking on my nipple as I squeeze slightly and gasp.

"Every time I'm around you," I confess out loud.

I keep that hand playing and teasing my nipple and then move my other hand down to my clit, I rub circles on it and gasp even louder.

I have never played with myself intimately but now I curse myself because of how good it felt. I rub rough circles on my clit biting my bottom lip.

"I need to taste you princess, to see if you taste as sweet as you act." I hear Aerilyn's voice in my head and my head quickly nods at the voice. I envision her mouth on me teasingly at first but then she starting licking me as if I were her last meal.

"Act? What act?" I ask but quickly finish with a moan as I buck my hips up into my hand, but in my mind, I buck my hips on Aerilyn's tongue.

"Well Arabella, you act so sweet but tonight you're being so naughty for me and Val. Will you let us ruin you?" Her voice in my head asks and not even two seconds later I nod my head quickly.

I pinch my nipple even harder with my left hand and push a finger into me with my right hand. I thrust it in and out of me slowly at first, knowing Aerilyn she would make sure to be slow with me until I was ready.

The slow pace was pleasurable but I needed more, more, and as if she heard me, I entered a second finger instinctively my walls felt so tight around my tight fingers. I keep moving them, pumping in and out of me. I felt myself stretch around them.

"So tight princess, we will have to fix that to accommodate Val." Aerilyn's voice says, her words was almost enough to finish me, my head lay back on the pillow as I keep the movement going.

The hand on my nipple moved over to my other breast and I pinched it so tight. It causes me to wince. It hurt but I couldn't stop the wave of pleasure building within me, the hand keeps defiling my breasts, I worried that they will be swollen.

I keep my eyes closed imagining Val's topless body next to me. He looks at me with the same look I saw in the room. He plays with me and there was no worry about rules in his eyes.

The hand in my pussy pumping in and out of me, starts moving faster and rougher. My back arches, I could see her lay on her stomach in front of me a wild grin on her lips as she slowly bit her lip looking up at me with lust in her eyes.

"I can't, I'm going to," I couldn't finish my sentence as I gasp at the feeling of release in me ready to explode.

The hand which was on my breast moves to my neck squeezing slightly, I imagine Val's face moving close to mine.

"No, princess I want your eyes open when you come. Be a good girl and look at me," he orders.

Arabella: These feelings

I couldn't say no, I feel as if I need to open my eyes. To follow his demands. I see his face close to mine, our noses close as I release all over my hand moaning so loud I worry anybody outside the room could hear. I squeeze my eyes shut the pleasure felt overwhelming, I pant heavily as if I had run a mile.

When I open my eyes I was back to my senses, I was alone in my room my hand was a mess with my own come. I scrunch my nose in disgust and go into my bathroom to wash my hands.

I look into the mirror to see my cheeks flush, and then the realization hit me as if a house had fallen onto me. I was falling in love with my best friend and my knight, the two people that was probably having sex with each other in a room not too far away from where I had played with myself. I clear my throat and shake my head, I quickly go back into my bedroom and crawl into bed pulling the covers over my head. A wave of emotion hit me as I put my hand to my erratic heart.

It took a while but I eventually fell asleep my mind stuck on Aerilyn and Val.

Valin: Damned Temptress

I felt as if my skin was boiling this afternoon. My focus was shifting and split. I was once so focused on Arabella and her well-being. Now today I almost lost the challenge because I was also thinking of Aerilyn.

I watch her walking with Sir Keiran. Her hands on his arm. Her smile towards him made me sick to my stomach. I try to shake off the feeling and focus on winning, but the damned guy was the one I was fighting.

I had not stopped to look at Arabella or Aerilyn afterwards. I did not even go to the after party. I stormed back to my room. There were maids coming in offering to help with any wounds I may have, but I did not want to be touched. Or I wanted to be touched, just not by them. I was fine, other than a few bruises that were starting to form.

I get out of the bath and dry off. I still had this burning feeling in my chest. It felt like it was staying. Thoughts of Keiran's words and Aerilyn were eating at me in ways I did not think was right. I should not care, but I did.

Valin: Damned Temptress

I put on a pair of clean pants and a shirt. I took no time to tuck it as I swing my door open and leave. A sudden rush of cold sensation course my body as I hesitate where I was going. The twinge in my neck was the last of my uncertainty as I knock on Aerilyn's door.

There was a moment before I almost turn and leave but the door opens. Aerilyn was still in her dress from this afternoon. I look behind her and double check the sun was down. It was dark, and she was not in her usual robes.

The glass of wine that was glued to her hands by this time was not. Her dress is ruffled and I try not to think about his hands, possibly one on her, to cause that. She looked up at me with wide surprise eyes. Her deep brown eyes that made me think of the sweetest of chocolate. There was a quick look of shock that turned into something else. *She seems to be putting up her walls.*

"Good evening." I was starting to doubt my choices for showing up here tonight. She looks shocked at seeing me. *Maybe she was waiting to seeing someone else.* That thought alone stirs me again.

"Good evening? Valin, did you need something?" She started to turn, looking around the room behind her. "Did you leave something earlier this morning?"

When she turns to face me again, there was a flush that was starting to raise from her chest to her cheeks.

"Can we talk?" The question sounds alien. She steps aside and makes room for me to walk in.

As I walk in, my eyes catch the steam off her bathwater. It looks to be freshly drawn. I was about to leave, but she walks past me and takes the bottle of wine that was on the table. She seems to be in no hurry to get rid of me, so I am probably over thinking this.

I sit on the couch with her. She pours two glasses and hands me one.

"You know I am not much of a wine person." I take a drink of it, anyway. The sweet taste that dances down with no burn.

"I know, but drinking alone is never enjoyable. It's not like it is bad tasting, though."

"No," I clear throat

"Just give it to me,"

"Give what?" She looks to be tense, like something bad was going to happen.

"You came to see me. You never come to see me. What is it?"

I nervously rub the back of my neck and set the wineglass down. Coming to see her seems so dumb now, but I think of her with Keiran and the doubt swims away.

"Why were you with Keiran?" I watch her blink up at me a few times. She takes a drink before responding.

"Does it matter?" There was that damn lip bite after she said her words, which flew out of her mouth.

"It does."

"He wanted to walk with me and make sure I was not by myself while the tournament was going. He was being thoughtful." Every word came out of her like a matter of fact. The playful Aerilyn looks to be dying in front of me. Someone that was starting to harden to the world around them.

"Do you seek his time?" I had to know. She did not waste her time with people she did not find enjoyment with.

"Possible." She was playing a game now. The light in her eyes starts like a fire. There was a smile that plays on her lips with the word like she was toying with me. I found myself drawn to her like a moth to a flame. I wanted to covet that flame.

To make it sacred, allow no one else to touch it. I gravitate towards her, to dare to get closer but not touch yet.

"Is that who you were waiting for tonight?" I watch her bite that damn lip.

"I was waiting for no one tonight." I could not tell if she was lying, but her gaze drink me in with bated breath.

"Do you do that with him, too?" One of her legs moves over my lap so casually. I run my hand up her dress. Feeling the soft skin of her thigh. She drank the rest of her wine before looking at me, dumbfounded.

"Do what?" I remove my hand from her thigh and take her glass to set it down. Turning back and lean into her more. I take her chin and see her hold her breath as I drag my thumb alone on her lower lip. Making her lips part, thoughts of lips round my cock have me pulsating with need.

"You have beautiful lips." My own voice is thick and laced with desire. I lean down and run the tip of my nose along her neck. She opens herself to me, as I take in the smell of her. The smell reminded me of the sea and sky.

I make my way up to her face. She licks her lips in anticipation, leaving them parted for me. I lean down to take her lips and stop. Thoughts of leaving start to come. How we should not be like this.

Her hands made their way to my face. Forcing me to look at her. The look of carnal desire danced with need in her eyes. She pulls me to her. The clumsy, raw desire of the kiss was breathless, and I wanted more. I want to feel her body on mine. Without the restraint of clothes.

"Gods, I need you so bad." She pants for much needed air. I felt I had no need for meaningless things. I wanted more. Moving down to her neck, holding her waist flesh to me.

Racking my teeth over her neck and reward it with slow kisses. Her moans fill the room, dancing between the walls.

"Then have me," she says through bated breaths. I groan, hearing her words of approval and feeling her grind her hips against me. Knowing she needs the release as much as I want it.

Her hands, desperate, grips the hem of my shirt and pulling it over my head. I suck in a breath, feeling the soft of her hands roaming over the bare of my skin.

I move my hands behind her, trying to unlace her dress. I remember seeing them earlier today. The thin strings snapping as I tug. The anguish need to feel her on me was too much to bear. I sit up to help the mountains of fabric over her head. Then, disregarding the rest of our clothes.

There was a moment of stillness as we sit. I open my mouth to say something, and she leans over to silents me with her lips. The wild look of untamed nature rages in her eyes. There was a small push of her hand and I follow leaning back on the couch.

She straddles my lap and reaches between us. Taking my full length and making slow, torturous strokes. My mind clouds. I moan for the need of more. To be able to feel while I drive deep into her.

There was a sudden stop and someone knocking loudly on the door. She scrambles to her feet and ran to where her robes were laying on the chair.

"One minute!" She yells. Her hair is mused and cheeks are flushed, showing exactly what was occurring. I get up just as quickly, throwing on my pants and shirt. I stood by the fireplace waiting for this person to walk in.

Aerilyn walks to the door and opens it as she finishes tying the robe. Her head maid comes in with a questionable look as she looks between Aerilyn and myself.

I clear my throat, take the bottle of wine and head for the door before questions could arise.

"Goodnight, Aerilyn." There was a mutter that came from her, but I did not wait to walk out the door.

Arabella: Feelings

I take a book from my bookshelf and sit on the bed. I open it and begin to read it. Four lines down, I stop and sigh, closing the book once again. I couldn't concentrate. The emotions I feel in my chest were swirling around in my chest: jealousy, curiosity, arousal. The moment I felt arouse, I shake my head. I turn my body to half lie hanging off the bed.

"Think Arabella, with your head," I say out loud. I was hoping all the blood would rush back to my head so I could think clearer. Then there was a knock at the door. I sigh, not wishing to see anybody right now, but maybe this would be a good distraction.

"Come in!" I shout, not bothering to move from my position. The door opens and in walks Aerilyn holding a bottle of wine and two glasses as per usual, *and hello distraction,* my brain jokes.

"Drinks? I thought you might need some after the stress of the fight today at the tournament?" she said as she sat down in the lounge. "You coming?" She asks, throwing a look over her

Arabella: Feelings

shoulder.

I quickly sit up, instantly regretting it with the whiplash I give myself. I look at Aerilyn confused and a little flushed when she said coming.

"Me? Coming? There's no coming in here." I clear my throat and sit up straight. "Coming where?"

"To sit here and drink with me. Are you okay? Do I need to leave?"

"Leave? No, no need everything is fine" I elongate my words at a higher pitch than I had meant to, I stand up and move over to the chair next to her. I stare at her for probably too long, trying to see if I could see any changes on any part of her skin that was bare. I couldn't see any marks *okay, so he isn't a rough lover then.*

"Are you sure you are okay?" She asks, reaching across and brushing her hand over my face.

The feeling of her touch is soft. It took every ounce of strength in me to not lean into it. I clear my throat.

"Yes, I'm fine, nothing a little wine won't fix." I smile at her, hoping it was enough to convince her that everything was okay.

She pours me a cup and hands it to me.

"You must be happy Valin won? You looked conflicted, though. Why?"

"Conflicted? Kind of, I have had some thoughts about his decision to enter, and I have a feeling this isn't what he really wants." I look down at the glass of wine swirling the drink around to keep me from looking at her.

"Oh, but he seemed determine when I talked to him."

"Things can change in the matter of days or even hours, can't they?" I say quietly and look up at her finally.

"I am sure, but have you asked him? Did he say something

that puts uncertain thoughts on you?"

"No, he hasn't said much to me, but actions speak louder than words sometimes. I did want to have this conversation with you last night, but I couldn't seem to find you," I say curiously. I lift the glass to my mouth, taking a sip, my eyes looking into hers.

"Oh, strange, I was just in my room, I think."

My eyebrow twitched in annoyance. I wasn't going to get an answer out of her. I put the glass down on the table and sit back to look at her. My elbow rests on the back of the chair as I lean the side of my head on my hand.

"I saw you last night, Aerilyn."

"Oh, I thought you could not find me? Why did you not visit?"

"Visit? Aerilyn, I *saw* you both, Valin, in the room last night, you left the door open," I express.

"Us both? That was, Nothing happened."

"Aerilyn," I say and pause for a moment trying to find the right words "I was worried you may have lost your tongue in his mouth you were both going at it like it was the end of the world, I wouldn't call that nothing"

"A slip of a moment happens from time to time with too much wine. This," She hold up her glass. "Is my first so I should be on good behavior. I am sorry I did not mean it. It will not happen again."

"Do you have feelings for him?" I ask. I could hear the jealousy in my voice, but I couldn't help it. "And please tell me the truth"

She took a drink before answering, but her face gave nothing away.

"No, I should not have done that. It was my fault."

Arabella: Feelings

I put my face into my hands and rub any tension I was feeling. Looking back to her moments later, after silence. I reach out and put my hand into hers softly.

"Aerilyn, people don't just kiss someone without feelings. Did something happen to upset you? I can help."

"Nothing happened." She finishes off her glass. Standing she, hovers over me, causing me to lean back. Her finger tips tracing the outline of my jaw until she tilts my chin to look up at her.

"I can kiss you now if you would like?" I gulp at the intense look in her eyes, but I didn't back away further from her.

"Kiss me? Then I would believe you have feelings for me if you do. Do you have feelings for me, Aerilyn?" Moving an inch closer to her, feeling a bit more daring. I look down at her lips, then back up to her eyes. I could feel her breath fanning my lips.

She leans down and meets my lips with hers. The soft gentle caress that whispers secrets to the unknown. I part my lips for her and she to took it greedily, only to pull back and look at me.

"I like the feeling of kissing, Arabella."

"I didn't like the feeling I felt when I saw you both kiss. If my eyes would show emotion, they would be a solid green"

"Then I won't be kissing him anymore." She pulls away. "If that is all, I think I might go to bed."

"I didn't mean to upset you Aerilyn," I stand up but don't move to stop her "but if you do feel something for him, then I won't stop you"

"I like to kiss. He just happened not to be the servant. I am fine Arabella. Everything is still the same for you and your knight, I promise."

To Be Damned

I want to stop her from leaving, to tell her the truth of my feelings, but the fear of rejection stops me. I clear my throat and place my hands together in front of me.

"Thank you for your honesty Aerilyn," I say in a formal tone. She left without looking back and without taking the wine bottle and glasses.

I stare at the door where she had left from. My heart aches. The longing feeling I felt was back the moment the door closes. I lie back on the chair and curl up, my knees bent to my chest as my cheek rests on the back of the chair as I slowly close my eyes.

Arabella: Ball of Nightmares

I stand at my father's side, nodding to each bowing guest that came into the room. There were violinists playing a soft tune, one that could easily put me to sleep. I was wearing a light pink dress one that was tied far too tight around my waist which I'm pretty sure was my father's orders to my lady-in-waiting to make me look more appealing to the guests especially the male ones that will be doing a tournament for my hand in marriage.

Once we welcome everyone inside, I take my leave in hopes I could get away before I had to dance with just about every man in here. However, my father had different plans. He puts a hand on my back and practically pushes me toward this older man. He looks older than my father is. I scrunch my nose but quickly recover and smile at this man.

"Your highness, I am Daedric Valor. It's so nice to meet you." he bows and then kisses the back of my hand. I want to vomit. He smells heavily of cigars and his touch was far less than gentlemanly.

"How lovely to meet you too, Sir Valor. We are to dance, yes?" I ask, hoping he was going to say no, but he grasps my hand and drags me onto the dance floor, almost causing me to tumble my back burns, feeling the heat of my father's glare from wherever he was. I know this embarrasses him when I wasn't 'the perfect princess'.

As we waltz on the dance floor, the crowd gathers to watch us some of the younger people laughing probably at my unfortunate circumstance and some cringing at how badly this man was dancing I wouldn't have called it dancing more like dragging me from one side of the room to the other and then breathing heavily causing me to almost vomit multiple times.

As the dance finishes, I bow as did he and before he could say anything I notice Aerilyn on the other side of the room, I quickly rush off towards her she was smiling at me but her eyes shown a pity look I shook my head.

"Don't say a word," I order her, even though she knew I was only half joking.

"I wouldn't dare princess, I will say he has gone straight to your father after that dance. I'm wondering if he's going to ask him for your hand," she jokes, making me cringe.

"Please don't say that. I'm not even sure it's possible that man can even give this kingdom an heir, so I'm sure father wouldn't say yes," I try to convince myself of my own words. My eyes glance over to where the man went and there he is, standing and talking to my father.

"I'm sure wherever you would go with him you would get a discount everywhere you go, him being over a certain age," she jokes, smiling widely at me. I chuckle and slap her arm playfully.

Arabella: Ball of Nightmares

"Not funny," I laugh, contradicting myself.

"Oh, and here's the next suitor" I turn around to see yet another older man. However, his eyes lingered on my chest and he holds out a hand to me. I turn to Aerilyn quickly, eyes wide. *'Save me'* I mouth to her and she gives me a sad, apologetic smile and shrugs.

"Sorry princess" she says and I groan quietly and turn back around to face this man I take his hand and he leads me to the dance floor *'well at least this one didn't drag me'* I think as he pulls me close to him by my waist I raise an eyebrow at his abruptness but he starts to sway.

There was no conversation just awkward swaying I feel his hand slowly lower to my behind, and I stiffen the nerve this man has I was about to call for the guards when I hear a cough behind us, the man let me go and turns around and we are met with Valin.

"I believe it is my turn, your Highness." I nod quickly at him.

"Of course," I reply, nodding to the man I was just dancing with and then I turn to Valin, slightly bowing to him. He puts his hand on his chest and bows at me. He did this every day, but seeing him in a fancier shirt and willing to dance with me causes me to blush.

He pulls me close to him. He pulls me close to him, with my right hand resting on his left and my left hand on his shoulder, while his right hand rests on my hip.

"I owe you," I smile jokingly, causing him to grin.

"It didn't look like you were having the most fun with him," he replies, moving us around the floor.

"So he does dance," I say in a mocking tone, smirking up at him. He grunts but couldn't stop the grin on his face.

"Is that how you treat the man that just saved you from an

older man trying to grope her? I am appalled, princess," he fakes being hurt by my words, causing me to laugh.

"How many drinks have you had? Because you're acting more friendly than usual," I ask as he twirls me and brings me back close to him, his arm curls around my waist even tighter.

"I am always friendly, your highness. But if you must know, I've had two drinks,"

The music stops and we pull apart, bowing to each other.

"Would you like to get some fresh air?" He asks, and I nod almost too eagerly.

"Yes please," my voice coming out more like a plead than anything else. He takes my arm and leads me out of the ballroom. We move onto a terrace overlooking the massive garden. I take a deep breath and close my eyes enjoying the cold air on my skin, goosebumps rose up when I feel Valin's presence right behind me I turn around to face him, he was close almost too close I take a step back till my back met with the balustrade. He moves closer and strokes my cheek with his thumb. I look up into his eyes. They were a darker green in this light. His stare was intense, but I couldn't look away.

"You look beautiful tonight, princess" I look at him in shock. I never got compliments from him, ever. I blush so hard and look down, embarrassed at how hot I was. His index finger moves to my chin, and he lifts my chin up to look up at him. His face was closer to mine now.

"You need to push me away princess other wise I may kiss you, and that's against my job description," he whispers, his eyes stare at my slightly parted lips. I bite my bottom lip.

"No, I won't push you away" that was all Valin needed before his lips met mine. It isn't a forceful kiss, it is sweet, passionate. I wrap my arms around his neck as his hands lie on my hips.

For what felt like seconds but was really minutes, we part and stare at each other.

"I have to go. I will see you tomorrow?" He asks, as if that kiss could be the end of his job. I mentally curse myself, remembering how much trouble he could be in if anyone saw what we did.

"Yes, tomorrow," I reply before he back away, walking backwards for a few steps, still staring at me, and then he turned and walked away. I put my fingers to my lips, stunned at what had just happened.

Valin: Night Alone

I had forced myself to pull away from the kiss. I did not even follow Arabella with the intent to kiss her, but to feel her lips on mine was all I could think about when she licked them. It was not something I should have done. I had my name in to try to win her hand, but to do that was the greatest sin I will cherish.

I had to leave because of the feeling of her against me. The feeling of the way her body fit into me was making my thoughts go into places other than kissing. I wanted to let my hand cup her neck, trail down her spine. I also wanted to continue being a gentleman that she may eventually grow to love, but I wanted to do things with her that would have taken that image away.

I cross the ballroom and left for my room. I wasn't running, but I was thankful for the long strides as my mind continues to wander. Thoughts of pinning her to the darkest corner and taste not only her lips but her delicate skin. Thoughts of what her moans might sound to my ears. The rush of what would come, knowing we might get caught.

Valin: Night Alone

Making it up the stairs, and walk down the hallway. I saw no one there but held the urge to touch myself. I was tortured. Tortured by the taste for wanting more. Tortured by thoughts of carnal desires. Desires that I have been so good at suppressing before now. But this was the first time I crossed all lines and allowed myself to touch those wicked lips.

I get past the last door around the corner. The door where the duchess was staying. I groan to myself as I start to think about her, too. She has been nothing but a temptress since arriving here.

Her door was closed thankfully. Maybe she was still at the ball. I hope she was. The last thing I needed was some flirty, snarky remarks. I pass her door and head down the stairs to the set of doors, which is my room.

I close the door and start to unbuckle my pants. There was nothing but relief as I release myself and start to stroke myself. I don't even make it to sit down as I lean against the door. The heat of my hand only fuels the need for release.

I close my eyes and think of the air kissing my cock, being the one from Arabella's breath. The feeling of her lips on mine traveling down as if she would want to be kneeling before me. I pulsate with need, thinking of her licking those lips before she would place it around me.

The thought has me tightening, begging for more friction. But I punished myself for going slow. To drag out the imagination of her. How I want to fist those pretty locks of hair. To slam down deeper into her mouth.

I grip my hair, in need of grabbing something with my free hand. I buck my hips and could feel my release building. My balls start to tighten just as I hear a knock on the door. In my delirium, I thought it was from me bucking for my release.

I continue to stroke but faster, not wanting to drag it out anymore. I can't help but moan as the sweet release washes over me.

I stand there panting, evidence of what just happened was on my shirt, hand, and floor. It helps some, but I still wanted more. I had taken off my shirt and washing my hands. I start to dry them when I hear the door start to be knocked again.

I freeze as I realize I did hear a knock at the door just moments ago. I clear my throat and throw the towel on the bed before answering the door.

I open the door and see Aerilyn standing there holding two chalice cups. Probably filled with red wine. She has a bad habit of drinking even more so when the sun is down. I don't say anything as I look her over. Holding those two chalices skillfully in her hand. Almost as if it was no big deal and not wearing her gown from the ball this evening. Her hair was let down and the look of boredom was on her face. She tilts her head higher and softly clears her throat.

"What do you want, Aerilyn?" I cross my arms and lean into the door frame. Blocking her entrance. *That would be the last thing that would be happening tonight.* I don't need any more temptations than there have been. She stood on her toes and tries to look over my shoulders.

"Got company?"

"No, and I don't need any." I start to move and close the door. The damn woman lost her balance and places her hand on my chest to catch herself. It would have been like any other time, but I had just taken off my shirt. The cool touch of her small hands causes me to freeze. Just long enough for her to slip inside.

I took a deep breath in and closes the door. It did not take

Valin: Night Alone

much to understand she was not used to being told no. She may not be a princess, but she is in her world. I turn and find her making herself home. My room was not as big as theirs, but I had everything they did. She sits on the couch and set the extra glass of wine on the table.

"How long have you been in here? You just sit in here without the fireplace started?" She chuckles.

"I have not been in here long. Not long enough to start a fire. I needed to cool off, anyway." I mutter the last of words, spoke for me alone.

I walk over to the fireplace and lit it up. Throwing a few logs in for good measure. *That would last for a few hours.* I sat down next to her, but there was a good amount of space. So much so that she drew her leg up in that space.

"What do you want, Aerilyn." She leans over, grabs the glass and hands it to me before answering. There was a mischievous smile that plays on her lips. For the briefest moment, there was that damn lower lip bite that she continuously does. I could feel the carnal desire coming back in full force. Like I did not just get done touching, stroking myself.

"So informal, Valin. What am I to do with you?" The sound of dare plays as a threat. A part of me wondered if she knew what she was doing. I have the suspicion she was not innocent like the princess, but the way she gave certain looks or said things made me wonder how much of a temptress she is.

"You are the one that showed up in a man's room after dark. I don't think you are looking for a formal meeting. So I will ask again, what do you want, Aerilyn?" I could have sworn there is a look of desire when I ground out her name. I did it more out of aggravation, but I would be lying if when I saw her close her eyes and shiver, a rush of excitement courses through me as well.

I tilt the glass back and drink the red liquid. The thick, sweet taste danced along my tongue and down my throat. I closed my eyes as I thought of how she must taste the same way. She always drinks this wine.

"I.." She pauses and I open my eyes to see her flush. "I don't know what I want. I just thought some company would be nice."

"You usually spend your nights with the princess. Why not tonight?" I finish the contents. Setting the glass aside, I knew that was probably too much to drink in one night as it was not my first drink. She stretches herself out and shamelessly lays her feet in my lap. For that, I found out she was not wearing shoes. The walk down the stairs alone must have been cold.

"I don't want her to grow tired of my presence." She was too comfortable sitting here with me, and I was not the man to be tested tonight.

"As much as I appreciate you thinking of me." I reach down and start to rub one of her feet. My thumb glides up the base and a moan slips from her lips. "I still don't think it is proper for a lady of your status to come this late to a gentleman's room."

There was a twinkle in her eye. That damn lip in her mouth again. Her tongue darts out, swiping along where she was biting. Only to take another sip before speaking to me again. I hate but loved catching every detail that she was giving me.

"Maybe I wasn't looking for a gentleman." Her words barely came out as a whisper. I am not even sure if she meant to say them. Either way, I heard them.

I move until I was hovering over her. Her eyes were frozen, not expecting me to move, but I was so damn tired of the tease.

Valin: Night Alone

I took her glass, drinking the rest of her wine. There was a sudden increase in her breathing and pulse, but she did not look as though she was scared away. Just the opposite. There was a sense of excitement and wonder about what will happen next.

I lean down and take that lower lip of hers. A gentle tug. I almost don't stop as she starts to wilt and whimper. The sound of her need makes me want to continue. To just have a taste.

Her hands start to snake around me. Pulling me closer to her. The clumsy crash of her lips to mine. The heavy taste of wine. I want to revel in this moment. To feel her skin on mine, but that taste of wine is so thick.

She was just drunk. I stop her and press my hand on her chest. She gives whimpers of pleas that did not help. Her robe was starting to fall off when she sat up after I did. Her hair looks a mess. I stand up and put some space between us.

"I think you should leave. Go to bed, Aerilyn." There was a pain in her eyes. The act of rejection she took personally and I can't blame her. But she kept her head high as she got off the couch, walks across the room. She left the room without the damn wine glasses.

Aerilyn: Practice makes Perfect

I stride along the hallway. My burgundy and creme evening gown swooshing with each step. My hands filled with a wine chalice in each. I did not have a drinking problem, but some liquid courage helps sometimes.

I get to the princess' door and, as if it is a routine, a new guard is posted to release Valin for the night.

"Aerilyn, what are you doing here?" Valin hesitated leaving. His green eyes start looking me over and back up.

"I'm here to have my late night fill of the princess. Good night Val!" I step in front of the door, waiting for the new guard to open it. When he did not, I look at him and see him looking between the two of us, trying to figure out if he was supposed to or not. I roll my eyes and turn to face Valin again.

"I am not here for anything more than girl gossip. Don't worry, she will have enough beauty sleep. Now," I turn to the guard. "Open the door." He clears his throat and follows his orders.

"Yes, your grace," he says.

Aerilyn: Practice makes Perfect

I walk in and kick the door closed behind me. Arabella jumps as if caught doing something. Whatever the something was, I was not sure, but her face was red. The maids have already helped her in pull down her bed, light her fire and dressed her in a golden lined evening gown. The robe ties were gold, but had a tassel that she was fidgeting with.

"Aerilyn, you startled me. Did you need something?" She asks, almost breathless.

"You? Always. Now I brought drinks and thought I would see if you found out about any of the competitors for this week?" I sit on the side of the bed and wait for her to walk over and take her glass.

She takes a few steps and takes the drink. I watch her look at it, swirl it and then drink deeply before sitting next to me. She holds on to the glass in her lap and lifts her feet to allow her toes to peek out over the hem.

"Do you want me to leave?" I ask because the silence told me that I was somewhere unwanted. She looks at me with her sad blue eyes.

"No, why would I want that? I am sorry. I just have a lot on my mind. I heard of a few suitors. Most of them are close to my father's age. I know they will be kind and take care of me, or at least I would hope. I think I held on to the idea that I would be able to choose and not be won off like a prized horse." I watch her eyes become very occupied with her toes and looked as if she was fighting not to cry.

"Well, let's change the subject and then we can come up with a plan to ruin the whole of this later. So what were you all red about when I came in here?" I reach over her lap and felt under her pillows. "What naughty book were you reading this time?" She starts to giggle and pushes me back up.

"I was not reading. I-" she presses her lips together. She starts to flush again and took another deep drink.

"I? What? You can not leave me hanging like to think!"

"Okay, fine, but you cannot tell anyone!" She finishes her drink and sets it aside. I watch her lift her dress as she pulls her leg onto the bed and faces me.

"Oh yes, I will gossip with all the maids and stable boys just to make sure the whole kingdom knew before the sun sets tomorrow." I roll my eyes and gave her a playful smirk behind my glass. She leans over and smacks my leg.

"Fine, I get it. But." She took a deep breath in and blows it out before talking. The wait making me more antsy. "I kissed a guy, and he is trying to win my hand." I froze but quickly try to find words.

"Kiss? That sounds serious." I try to make it sound playful, but it feels like acid on my tongue. "So, have you been seeing this guy for long? Do tell me, is that why you read those books? To practice when you can't be in person practice?" I give a laugh and I watch her go from stiff to she was laughing with me.

"No, well." I watch her bite her low lip. I resisted the urge to reach out and touch her, but also pushing her to answer faster. "I do read them to try to know, but no, I haven't with him."

"No?! You are lying!"

"No, I am not! When would I be able to, honestly?" She brings her foot on to the bed. Her big blue eyes fill with curiosity and she almost looked hesitate, but she shakes her head slightly. "What about you Aerilyn?" She blurts out the question like it was choking her.

"Oh, I have had lots of practice." I smile, watching her eyes widen in surprise.

Aerilyn: Practice makes Perfect

"How? Don't you get caught?"

"No, I am not noticed when missing. Helps to not be a princess. But.." I let the word trail off as I tip the rest of my wine back.

"But what?" The forever stain of blush was now from her cheeks and painted down her neck. I lean over her and place my glass next to hers. Forcing her to lean back on the pillows. I brush the tip of my nose long across her jaw and nip her earlobe. Her gasp was low in my ear. The heat of her breath blowing into it sends a wave of excitement down my spine and to my core.

"Practice can be with anyone. We could practice. You and I are in the perfect spot and no one would know. I could teach you a few things that I have learned" I run my finger along her collarbone and start to drip between her breasts but stop waiting hear her answer. Her breathing has become shallow and I'm tempted to take that as a yes.

I take a pillow and prop myself on the bedpost with the pillow behind me. Sitting directly in front of her. I let my legs fall open. A thrill of exposure was enough to make me wet.

"Here, show me what you learned from those books you said you read." Her eyes widened, but she plays the part of an innocent princess, all while turning red as an apple.

"What?" Her question almost chokes out of her.

"I want you to show me what you learned." I start to spread my legs. Making sure just enough material falls to cover my core, but let the rest spill off my legs.

"I would not know where to start."

"Oh sure, you do. Just follow my lead. I will teach and then we can work up the practice."

She looks to be conflicted. There is a pause before she looks up at me like a deer staring at a wolf.

"I don't know Aerilyn."

I get up and place a kiss on her cheek.

"Don't worry about it. If you need someone, let me know." I get off the bed and leave. Not giving her a chance to change her mind. She was not ready, and I was not going to push her.

Aerilyn: Now Is the Time

I have been following my Father's wishes and courting Sir Keiran. After the almost moment Valin and I almost shared, I have been vigilant to stay away from the temptation. I have not been visiting Arabella in the evening either, and she has been busy during the day.

There were only a few more days left before someone will win Arabella's hand. I felt I was running out of time. Time which is not rewarded me in this life to expend.

After getting ready for the day, I met Sir Keiran downstairs for breakfast. Like I have been for the last few days. This time he is not dressed for the tournament this day. I try not to look so surprise as I walk up and let him take my hand. He places a kiss on it like he does every day.

"You look absolutely beautiful, Aerilyn." He tells me as he pulls out a chair for me to sit.

"Thank you. You are not dressed for the tournament today?" There is movement as the servants came in with poached eggs and toast for the two of us.

"I thought it would be nice to take a step back today."

"Oh, why is that?"

"To spend it with you, of course." There was a small flush which came to my face as he spoke.

"Always so thoughtful." I whisper.

"Well, I think it is important because." He clears his throat and turns his body some more to face me more directly. "I have asked your father to take you home with me. I would like to have your hand in marriage." His eyes held a sense of seriousness and determination.

I hear his words and I could feel my heart beating faster. I feel the flush in my face deepening. He probably thought it was flattery. I was just sold off like cattle without the decency of a simple talk. I feel completely blindsided. Gripping my hands in my lap until I could feel some pain, I finally look up at him with a smile.

"I did not realize you fancied me so much that you are thinking that far in the future."

"It is really not that far. We leave in a week."

I blink a few times. I realize I had no idea what house he was. Entertained him for the sake of humoring my father, but never seemed to ask the simple questions like this.

"And you reside where? I don't think this has not come up?"

"Another neighboring island." He said it so nonchalantly.

I had finish picked at my food while he finished. There was silence, but I have nothing to say. I felt out of any sense of control and I could feel the rage brewing like a storm roiling in. I excuse myself from the table and tell him I would meet him later outside.

I walk up to my room. A small part of me wanted to be dramatic and cry on the bed. Which would help no one. The

Aerilyn: Now Is the Time

trunk I brought with me here was at the end of the bed.

I open the trunk and start taking out dresses. Once empty, I lift the hidden board and pull out my book. The book that holds so many of my secrets. Secrets I found in those woods.

I flip through the pages and make a pray to myself for real magic. A spell that the people are always scared of. I saw what I always did. Herbs. Medicine. Poison.

What was I doing? This was dumb. I close the book, hiding it away again. I was no witch and I would not hurt someone because I was not getting the things I wanted.

I get up and find my way to the wine cellar, I just need more wine.

Valin: Thank you

~~~~

There was a call for a meeting. A summons to the King's council room. I walk in, not in my uniform as I was getting ready for the last fight. All the members were sitting around the table, the king at the head and Sir Keiran next to the king.

This was the first time seeing him here, and he was someone I was going to fight with today. A small worry, that he had seen me with Aerilyn and me, deciding to tell the king that I need to be stripped of my title and competition. I keep my face neutral but prepare myself for what might come.

She was drunk, and I sent her away. There was nothing more going on. The thought made my heart ache. I should not being thinking about her. I should not have desired her the way I did.

Everything I have done led to this moment for the princess. It was she that I wanted. It was she that gives me comfort without so much as a touch on the coldest of nights.

I stand at the table like I always do. Hands clasped behind

Valin: Thank you

me.

The king looks around us.

"Good morning, as you all know. Today is the last day. I have some news from Sir Keiran, though." He gestures for Keiran to speak. Keiran pushes the chair back as he stands at the table.

"I am withdrawing from the tournament." There was a string of shocked breaths and murmurs among the men in disbelief.

"But why?"

"Has something happened?"

"What now?"

"Do we bring in the last contender that was disqualified?"

The questions did not stop and were growing louder. My own uncertain thoughts swirled. *What did that mean for me?*

"Enough," the king raises his voice over the growing chatter in the room and in my head. All attention snaps back to the King. Keiran starts back in as the chatter dies.

"I am courting someone else and did not think I would make it this far. It would not be fair to the princess to possibly win if I were courting another person." Leaving one to ask. Who? They did not need to ask for me to have a good guess who it was.

"Who are you courting? Why join at all if you did not want the princess' hand? You are not from our island, so did you not want a tie of political allegiance?" There was a smile from Gregory's lips. A smile that was unsettling to me.

"Aerilyn, from the Kenslyven house. She is someone I have had my eyes on. I have been in contact with her father for sometime now. I heard about your little tournament and I wanted to see how I would fare with your people. You all are known for your wealth and prosperity, but I wanted to see how your people fare in a fight. I am impressed to say. It was a kill two birds with one stone situation." He seems so calm, making glances at me. I listen to him and my blood boils. Undermining my work with the people on training and looking at Aerilyn. He wanted her.

"So now you leave and report your findings? What's next? You use it against us?" I say through gritted teeth.

"Oh, no, the opposite. In this kingdom, the people have proved to make a great alliance. I want to extend a hand even if I don't take the princess in marriage. The duchess is still part of your royal people, is she not?"

The king sits there, leaning back, and looks lost in thought.

"She is, so if she has a place at court, would she be our voice there?" The king questions. From a political stance, it was a good chess piece to move, but I did not like it. I did not want this.

"In time, yes." There was a sense of relief. Like there was time.

Time, but time for what? She would never be mine. Maybe time for her to demand something else? The king starts to sit up and had a look that he had made up his mind. Everyone stared at him, waiting in anticipation for what was to be next.

"Then it is decided, you withdraw from the competition to court the duchess. In the intent that you take her in marriage. Allow her to me our voice in your court. You have my blessing. Since you are no longer competing," the king looks at me. "You are the winner, Valin. Congratulations."

The growing murmurs started again.

"But Sire," the king raises his hand to shut the council man up.

"If this is to question my decisions, I will not have it. I have been questioned enough recently. Don't you think?" He was

Valin: Thank you

not threatening in words, but he emanated authority in his tone. The council man nodded in agreement but started to open his mouth to speak again.

"Yes, I agree. I was just going to suggest to at least announce it at the tournament. Maybe have something to entertain the people with, something else?" The king gave a slight pause. The look in his eyes said he already made it his mind, but giving the councilman grace to think over his request so he did not feel dismissed.

"That should be fine. And what do you suggest for an entertainment replacement?"

"Maybe have the rest of the other contenders come in for one last fight. The people loved it. The total chaos."

"That is fine, but Valin is exempt from it. I do not want him hurt or unnecessary injuries to occur." Everyone muttered their agreement. "Everyone is dismissed. Now leave." He dismissed us and, unlike any other time, I leave wanting not to speak right now.

My heart was pounding, and I wanted it to still. Talking was not going to help. I also did not want the king to think that I doubted my own decisions about his daughter. I have spent my whole life working for the position I have. To have this chance to have her hand was everything I dreamed of, so why was I concerned for someone like Aerilyn.

A duchess that is nothing but a temptress. She walks like no one notices her. She drinks way too much wine like this is no room for concerns for tomorrow. Damned woman with her damned lip biting. Someone who is trouble and should not have me this worked up.

This might be good. Have someone else give her the attention she so desires but not ask for. I found myself walking to the princess' room. Owen was standing outside the closed door. I open it, not knocking. She was sitting in the lounge, reading one of her many books.

She looks up at me with shock. A faint blush paints across those soft innocent cheeks. She gasps my name in surprise, but not unwelcome. I walk over to her and capture her lips with mine.

The soft touch, our touch something not of fight but like two partners in a dance with a slow crescendo. Something that was addictive but not born from desperation.

I cup the back of her neck, and she wraps her arms around me. Something so damn perfectly fit between us. How could I want more?

I lay my forehead on hers and listen to her soft pants. She dared not to ask for more. How would she know how to? I breathe in her rose petal scent and let it settle my racing heart. Letting it fill me, but there was a hole that was still there. A dull ache that I was trying to ignore.

"Thank you, princess." I say, as I place another kiss on her lips. One much softer. There was a soft whimper of discontentment and her blue eyes looked at me with confusion. Not just confusion, but a sense of desire she wanted to explore.

I could not bring myself to tell her I won. She would find out soon enough. Today I will stand in front of the people as the King announces it. I will take my place at her side and make sure she shines with joy.

"You're welcome, but I am not sure what you are thanking me for." She says as she starts to stand in front of me. Her body begging to be touched again. It was a mistake, something too soon, again. I had to know. I had to make sure nothing had changed.

Valin: Thank you

I brush her soft cheek with my knuckles, and I watch her shiver with delight.

"Just thank you. I will see you later today. There is a surprise after the Tournament." I leave before she could ask me about it. Or about why I kissed her again. I left before she could see my own torment, even though I was happy.

I walk out of her room and Owen stared at me with his judgment gaze.

"What?" I said, harsher than I intended.

"Was that really necessary?" Was the only words that came out.

"Yes," I stormed out before he could cast anymore of his holy judgment.

Aerilyn: I understand

I am sitting at my vanity. The maids have not come in to help me dress for the day, but I can manage my hair and makeup. Just getting through brushing my hair when someone comes through the doors. I was prepared to see the servant, but to my surprise, it was Sir Keiran. I hide my surprise and stay where I was sitting. My robe was open because I was ready to get dressed for the day. I cross it over me.

"Keiran, morning. Is there something important that it could not wait until breakfast?" I turn slowly on my vanity bench and see his better. He looks to be to calm. Something was off, but I could not say it didn't excite me.

"I heard something, and I want the truth." My brows knit, but I nod my head in understanding. I was taken aback by his words, which had a tone of seriousness that I was not accustomed to with him.

"I heard that there may be something going on with you and the Princess's personal guard. The Captain of Guards."

I want to play it off. To pretend there was nothing going on.

Aerilyn: I understand

That I was the perfect little future which he possibly looked for in me. I start to stand and hold my head up, but the look in his eyes said he knew. He looks mad, but I expected furious. No man wants a used woman for a wife.

He closes the distance between us. There has not been a moment that I desired this man, but something about him at this moment made me feel a momentary weakness. He grips my waist and pulls me into him. Not allowing space at all.

"I don't care about the details, but I want someone to put an end to it."

"Okay, I understand." I did not know what to say. To stop a wildfire was impossible, but I could see it bothered him.

I did not understand this budding blossom that was between us. One which grew over time until the storm that was brought with the other two. Leaving here would be good to nurture this to grow. He has been nothing but kind and caring.

It was not like he was an unsightly man. I just thought I would want more. The more I see, this is not going to end well for me. I could not let this be my story.

A woman as a mistress of the future king or queen. One to warm their beds but never seen.

Standing here with Keiran, I could see now I would not be a piece of jewelry put on until it is a convenient for him.

The grip on my arms turns to something softer. The air between us being one which was lighter. His hands transform into a touch of desire. Pulling my waist in and tilting my chin to look at him with his other.

There was a swirling emotion of desperation dancing in his eyes. A plead to see him. One that I have not been doing, because I was too busy chancing something I could not have.

"I will make it my goal to give you all the happiness. I know

To Be Damned

I am not the most daring man. I know I am not your first pick. I know you dream of things this world can not offer you, but I will do everything in my power to fight for you. To fight for your praise. To fight for those fires in your eyes to burn for a simple man like me. I will set you on a throne and gladly bow to you, Aerilyn. If you would only allow me."

His lips brush against my lips, waiting for my response. I was so conflicted in my heart, but I knew what I needed to do. It did not make it any easier to finally do it.

I close my eyes before meeting his lips with mine. Ones that are gentle. One met with love and adoration. They promised me the security I desire, or the world if I only ask for it.

I part my lips, opening myself to him. Giving a part of myself that I would not dare with Valin or Arabella before. He takes it graciously and leaves me weak. The defense I have perfectly curated was being chipped down, but this man. It would be a long time before it was completely gone, but for whatever reason, I trust him.

He grips the fabrics that clung to my waist but broke our kiss. Laying his forehead on mine. The silence that is deafening but somehow a solace of our own.

"I understand." I tell him again. He places a kiss on my forehead, but I could not tell if he believes me. Maybe he pretends to just like I pretend it. Pretends I could stay away from them like the need for air in my lungs. That as long as I was on this island, they would not be my darkest temptation. I was lying, and he was allowing it.

It was not one that I was proud of. He knew just like I did, soon I would be gone and there would be no more distractions. Maybe he hoped to win my heart after that. One which is locked behind a thorn bush.

Aerilyn: I understand

He steps out of our embrace and starts to leave. He stops on the threshold and looks up at me. I hold myself, afraid I might break.

"I stepped out of the tournament. That means Sir Valin will win." He searches my face after saying his name, but I keep my head high.

"Just as he should. They will be perfect together." I said with certainty. With that, he left. Satisfied.

Arabella: Champion

An unexpected summoning from my father has me on edge. It sounded serious and my mood went from being happy from the kiss this morning to fear of what this was about. The last day of the competition was almost here, Valin against Keiran. Just the thought of that fight made me feel like I was ready to vomit.

I follow Owen to the library, which makes me even more nervous. Father never summoned me to the library. It was always either the throne room or his private quarters, but never the library.

Owen opens the door for me and I walk in, seeing my father in the center holding a book and staring at it intently, as if it holds all the secrets. I walk closer and as soon as he puts the book, *The Missing Piece*, down; he looks up at me, the stress on his face fading into a smile when he sees me.

"You called?" I meant it to be a statement, but I was so nervous about the summoning that it came out as a question. I move over and sit at the seat by the table he is standing at. He sits in front of me and hums happily. His eyes look at the book, then back at me.

"One of the happiest moments of my life was when you were born. You brought so much light into mine and your mother's world." he stops for a moment, trying his best to keep his composure. "If she was still here, I know she would be so proud of you as am I"

"Father, where is this all coming from? Are you okay? Is your health declining?" The questions came out of me quicker than what I meant for.

"I am fine, I promise. A competitor has dropped out of the competition and so now we have a definite winner," I freeze wondering if it was Valin who dropped out of my brain wondering if he wanted Aerilyn instead of me if she was who he chose and if that was the case then I would have to marry Keiran I couldn't picture myself with him. "Sir Keiran has made the decision to drop out of the competition. He wants to court somebody else, meaning Valin has won and you two are to be married" he explains and watches my reaction carefully as if determining if I was happy or sad about this news and honestly I didn't know how I felt about it. On the one hand, I was happy to be marrying Valin, someone I admired since I met him, someone who protected me. But on the other hand, it didn't take much for me to realize who Keiran wanted to court. All he could do was talk about Aerilyn when I talked to him. Would *she agree to his courtship?* I put on my best smile and look up at my father.

"How did Valin take the news?" I ask, placing my hands in my lap.

"How I would have expected him to he was quiet I think it came a shock to him too. But I think he's happy and he will make a great king and husband," I smile softly at his words. It was a lot to take in, but in a good way.

"Was there anything else?" I ask.

"Valin will meet you later. He has a surprise for you," he smiles.

I stand up and kiss his cheek. I turn to walk away and Owen opens the door again for me, but I stop beside Owen. Slowly turning around and look at my father "You know, mother would be proud of you too" I see his eyes water but before I could see his tears, I walk out of the door.

Arabella: Name Day Celebration

I watch the hustle and bustle outside, everybody is rushing about with bunches of flowers they all had excited looks on their faces. My fathers words play in my head Valin won the competition then he came to me and kissed me. My hand moves up to my lips still feeling the touch of his lips on mine. I ponder on why he kissed me, was he happy he won or was it him seeing if I was what he wanted still?

A knock at the door knocks me out of the daydream I was having watching everybody outside.

"Come in" I shout, the door opens and to my surprise it was Val on the other side, I look at him and my cheeks redden instantly remembering the kiss we shared merely hours ago.

"Princess-"

"Arabella," I interrupt him, I cross my arms and purse my lips "it's Arabella when we are alone" I remind him. He doesn't reply to my statement.

"I came to inform you that preparations are almost finished for tonight, I convinced your father to let you out of the castle walls for a name day celebration, providing you stay close to me at all cost" he says and the world seemed to slow. He remembered how much I was struggling being locked in the castle, remembered what I do desperately wished for.

I feel my eyes fill with tears I rush over to him and wrap my arms tightly around his waist, my head resting on his chest. For a moment he stiffened, he looks over his shoulder to make sure no one could see us. But then he places an arm around my back.

"I'm guessing this means you are happy?" He asks a cheeky smile on his face causes me to laugh. I step back and quickly wipe my eyes.

"I am very happy yes, Thank you Valin this means a lot."

"Your welcome princess" he smiles "I'll see you at the carriages" he says bowing to me and then walks out of the room.

Once the door is fully shut I couldn't help myself from jumping up and down on the spot excitedly, I run to the window and look outside, my brain could only imagine how the town looked these days, but now I'm going to see it with my own eyes.

My maids came in shortly after to help me into a comfortable pale pink dress and some flat pumps insisting anything with a heel would be horrible to walk in our on the cobbled streets, I think I prefer the comfortable pumps over the tight uncomfortable heels they normally make me wear.

They add a small amount of makeup to my face to give me a healthier glow.

Someone knocks on the door and instead of shouting for them to come into the room I skip to the door and open it myself. Val was stood there in his uniform, he smiles.

"You look beautiful princess, are you ready to go?" He asks

and I nod with excitement. I shut the door behind me and he leads me outside where there are carriages with horses.

I grin and walk over to where the horses were stood, there was a huge white horse with specs of gray on him. I slowly place my hand on his nose and stroke it softly, his nose moves forward and nudges my cheek causing me to laugh. I love the horses but not being able to go out of the palace walls I never got to see them often.

"Are you ready princess?" I hear Val ask, I turn to look at him he was holding the door open to the carriage, I take a deep breath and nod, I walk over and take his hand as he helps me in, I sit down next to the window on the other side. A moment later Aerilyn gets in with help from Valin and I smile widely at her.

"I'm so glad I get to experience this with you" I muse as the door shuts.

"I wouldn't miss it for the world Arabella, do you think they will have wine?" She asks me making me laugh.

"They will definitely have wine, it's a party" I look out of the window as the carriage starts moving. It was a slow journey as Valin walked next to the carriage to keep both an eye on me and on anything suspicious outside.

The town was beautiful, the buildings were tiny in comparison to the castle but just looking at them all I felt was cozy, I imagine myself living in one of them, being a regular girl. The imagination ended very quickly when I see crowds of people cheering, I feel my cheeks heat with shyness but I smile through it and wave through the carriage window, there were many people dressed in their best clothes, some people had stems of roses which they held out to me.

Further into the town the carriage finally stops, the door

opens and Aerilyn stands first and Valin helps her out. I stay where I was and keep looking out of the window, I take a deep breath and move over to the carriage door Valin takes my hand as I get out. I look around seeing a throne at the top of stone steps, it overlooks a lot of the towns folk they were clapping and cheering at my arrival. I wave at all of them and let Valin leads me up to where the throne was, I sat down as he stood next to me. I watched as people danced with each other, there were people eating at a food table, and someone was lighting oil lamps making it a beautiful scene. I see Aerilyn with a glass of wine and I grin shaking my head, that woman and her wine were always inseparable. As if she had felt my stare on her she turned to look at me, she put her wine on the table and walked up the stairs to me.

"Come dance princess" she orders holding her hand out to me I look to Valin he nods at me.

"Just stay close, both of you" he orders to us, causing Aerilyn to scoff.

"So bossy" she jokes and pulls me up and drags me to the crowd of people and we dance in circles, holding hands spinning each other around. Once the violins had finished we stood and bowed at each other.

I carry on dancing in the crowd of people enjoying the music and being around others, occasionally I would catch Vals eyes, I would grin and keep dancing till my feet would hurt.

I walk to the food table to grab something to eat. I look at all the foods and I wasn't sure what would be good to try.

"The finger sandwiches are always a safe choice" I hear and smile. Turning around Val is stood there with his arms behind his back.

"Finger sandwich it is" I grab one at random and bite into it moaning at the meaty flavor hitting my tongue, I saw Val gulp but then pretends to look elsewhere as if something else was more interesting.

"Why don't you dance?" I ask once I finish the sandwich.

"I don't really dance" he simply says, "but it is your name day princess, I have something for you" he says and reveals a picture, I took it from him and see the most beautiful drawing of me, I was surprised it looked so realistic, I look up at him.

"Did you do this?" I ask trying not to cry, it's been too much of a emotional day already.

"I had help from an artist but I felt you needed to see what others saw, not a princess trapped in a castle but a future queen waiting to strive" he explains and that was all it took, a tear falls down my cheek, his thumb moves to wipe it away.

"I love it, Thank you" I say and go on my tiptoes forgetting where we were. I go to kiss him but he moves his head to make me kiss his cheek. Clearing my throat I take a step back, I knew and understood why he rejected the kiss but it didn't stop the embarrassment or hurt it felt.

"Princess, I-"

"No need Sir Valin maybe you should go find Lady Aerilyn and make sure she hasn't gotten too drunk." I interrupt, my voice had been so monotone, it was petty and I wanted to apologise but I didn't. I turn away from his surprised face and smile at a group of children dancing.

"It's the princess!" one of them shouts. I smile at them all.

"I was wondering if you all would honor me with a dance?" I ask smiling at them.

They grin and nod, we held hands and I copy a lot of their silly moves that they had. They laugh at my attempts obviously I wasn't terribly good at their moves. Once the songs finish, I talk to them about the town they told me about their favorite places that they go to. Eventually their parents came to take them home for bed, it was getting terribly late.

I look around for Valin to see if we had to go but I couldn't see him. I frown and move out of the crowd.

"Valin?" I shout looking left to right, there was no sign of him. I move further out across the cobblestone, there was still no sign. Anxiety filled me worrying if something happened, until I hear a moan to my left. I look into a slightly ajar tent and see Valin and Aerilyn kissing and touching each other hungrily, it was almost as if they needed to touch every part of each others body otherwise they would die.

I shake my head and look to the picture in my hand that Val had given me, I did tell him to go to Aerilyn. I turn to walk away when I feel someone behind me, I tense up feeling like something or someone was close behind me. I gulp and attempt to run but a hand clasps over my mouth. I tried to scream but the hand muffled the screams. I thrash my arms trying to elbow the person. I got one good strike in causing the person to hiss, it sounds like a man. The hand was big and the arm felt muscular. I just needed to get his hand off my mouth to scream and get Val's attention.

I try to bite the hand on my mouth but he quickly changes hands, the hand that was now on my mouth had some form of white cloth around it, and once it was against my mouth and nose, my vision starts to spin, my body was getting weaker and weaker almost as if I was drunk.

I feel the picture fall out of my hand onto the floor. I wanted so desperately to get it back, I felt everything go black and I fell into the strangers arms. His fingers stroke my hair softly and the last thing I remember was his voice.

Arabella: Name Day Celebration

"I found you."

Valin: Chokehold

I went through the motions after seeing the princess today. Her eyes light up with an explainable amount of joy, but my eyes wander to Aerilyn. She wasn't even looking at me. She was smiling and laughing with Gregory. I should be happy but I could not shake this feeling.

The people start lighting the oil lamps in the street and I made the princess promise to stay close to me. I had a few guards posted about, but there were so many people. They were happy to see their princess. She was so worried not so long ago about not being here with them, and it was like no time had passed. She underestimated their love for her.

They were starting to dance and pulling her in. She asked me to join her, but I was not one with clever footing. My heart was not in it right now either, but I was not about to tell anyone that. I had done well to avoid Aerilyn, but I could not help but look to catch a glance at her.

She was weaving through the people with her damned wine. I saw no signs of Keiran, though. I look away. She is not my

Valin: Chokehold

concern.

The sun was almost gone from the horizon by the time one of my men came up to me.

"Sir,"

"Yes?"

"It's Aerilyn, I think someone needs to take her back to the castle."

"Then go do it. Or find Sir Keiran to do it." I say with more irritation than I meant for. I see the princess going to a stand that had some kind of finger foods.

I walk up behind her and ask something about finger sandwiches.

"Finger sandwich should be safe," I confirm

"Finger sandwich it is." She said all to chipper and took it in a bite. Only to then moan at the flavors, the same moan I imagine she would do with me.

"Why don't you dance?" She asks me yet again but this time not adding the 'with her'.

"I don't really dance, but it is your name day, princess. I have something for you." I pull out the picture I had made for her. She looks up at me with wide eyes and almost in tears.

"Did you do this?" Her voice cracks with emotions.

"I had help from an artist, but I thought you needed to see what others saw. You are not the trapped princess, but a future queen." I try to explain without it sounding weird and see she is now crying. I move without thinking and wipe her tears away.

"I love it, thank you." She stands on her tiptoes like she wanted to kiss, but there were people here. I may have won her hand, but all eyes were on us now and so I turn my head so she could place the kiss on my cheek. I turn and see the reject and hurt in her eyes.

"Princess, I-" I try to find the words, but they were lost.

"No need Sir Valin. Maybe you should go find Lady Aerilyn and make sure she hasn't gotten too drunk" The formal tone came out. She dismissed me without using that phrase and left into the crowd of children dancing.

My same guard came up again.

"What?" I snap

"She won't allow anyone to touch her. Sir Keiran is nowhere to be seen." I sigh deeply.

"Okay, I will take care of it." I step away and look for Aerilyn in a tent they said she was in. She had enough. She was there, curled up and drunk. Damned woman.

I walk over and take her drink. Only to pour it out on the ground.

"Hey! That was mine! Get your own to waste!" She stands, but grabs my armor to steady herself. Her words coming out a bit of a slur. She was drunk, but not as bad as my men let on.

"Sober the hell up or go inside. This is not the time for this." Her expression hardens.

"No, I am getting more to drink. It is a celebration, is it not?! You and the princess are to be happily married, riding in the sunset. Oh, it's her name day." She drug out the word name. It was drunken spite, but why? She was about to get what she wanted.

"What are you going on about? What do you want?" I was so tired of guessing any of this. I was so tired of reading people, I just wanted someone for once to spell it out for me.

"It doesn't matter what I want. It never has." She tries to leave to go drink more. The damn drinking that was one day going to be the death of her.

"Maybe not." I grab her and make her face me. "But humor me."

"I want things that this world deemed I am not worthy enough to have."

"Is that why you continuously drink?"

"Yes, I don't want to feel anymore. I want to feel anything but the nagging reminder that I am not good enough for her. Or have you?"

I was shocked at hearing her words. Maybe a part of me knew. I knew she was overly close to the princess but to desire her, but then to also want me.

"You want us both?"

"Don't you mock my desires, Valin. I see the way you look at the princess and what you did to have her. I also am no idiot to see how you are with me the minute you get any alone time. You have wicked desires just like me. Just how far does yours go?" Her heated words coming out as she started to build more walls. Her hands like fist laying my chest, ready to start hitting me if I said the wrong thing.

I grip her chin and make her look up at me properly before I slam my lips to hers. Moans of desperation were coxed in coals of fires. To know she desires the same of me, gave me all I need to take from her. To take from the forbidden fires and stoke my own. To burn and welcome its warm embrace.

I could have spent the rest of the night in her arms. The want of more as she grips on to me like she might float away.

There was a shouting that causes me to stop. I hold on to Aerilyn's arm. I heard them say the princess was missing. The people in a complete chaos. I let go of Aerilyn and start to look around in a panic and seeing one of my men.

"Where is she?" I demand, holding on to his uniform.

"She went to look for you, I think, but no one has seen her. There was a strange figure that had someone that looked like maybe it was her dress. There did not think anything of it at first but went to follow them. The stranger knocked them out once they saw it was her."

"Who seen it?" He points to one of the town people that was already bruising around his eyes. The King came in,

"Where is she?" He sees me in his panic of fury. "You promised this would not happen. What happened?" I had no words. I was distracted, I had my eyes off her. He could see the guilt in my eyes.

"I don't know. I failed my job."

"Get out of my sight. Everyone else in my chambers now!" He turns towards the castle. The quiet somber turns to tears as the sky starts to cry with the hearts of the people.

Aerilyn: Caught in Feelings

I quicken my footsteps back to my quarters. I did not think I had the answers but I could not sit around like a helpless babe either. I did not hear anyone following me or see any signs either. I master not looking over my shoulders when sneaking around to make myself less obviously suspicious. In turn I learned to keen my hearing on the subtle sounds of footsteps but I did not hear them until I felt the grab at my wrist.

I almost scream, feeling the sound in my throat as I am spin around to face him but muffle the sounds by simply covering my mouth. I search his face realizing it is Valin. His eyes dark telling me there was no teasing and running away this time. Maybe if a guard came down the hall I could make enough noise to flag them but unfortunately for me they were all called forth to the king's chambers to come up with a plan to rescue the princess. The princess he was supposed to watch but wasn't because of me. I could see in his eyes he blamed me just like I was blaming me.

I take a deep intake through my nose trying to slow the threat of tears and settle my nerves. I close my eyes, smelling cedar, sweat and the linger of whiskey on his breath. A pang of guilt hit me in my stomach as I realize I found comfort in his smell. Sadness hit me as I was also the cause of the smell of whiskey on his breath.

His breath was ragged but began to slow. For the briefest moment his eyes were soft only to filter different darkened emotions.

"I was supposed to be there." His voice is rugged and fans my face. I close my eyes avoiding his death stare. I nod with the slightest movements against the palm of his hand.

He moves his hand and I reopen my eyes. He was looking down and his hand which was pressed against my mouth was starting to tremble. He looks as if he is about to burst. I gently took his hand trying to comfort him.

"I know. It was not your fault." *It was mine.* The last sentence was lodged somewhere in my throat not daring to spew into existence. A mocking half heart laugh comes out of him, dropping my wrist by my side and slamming his fist into the wall behind my head.

"And let me guess this is your fault then?" His voice croaks.

I move his shaggy hair that fell over his eyes with his sudden movement. Trying my best not to show my own hands trembling. I cup his face and my heart shattered as he flinches away from my touch.

"Come in. Sober up for a few moments." I said reaching for the door knob and opening it from behind me.

I lead him in by his hand and he seems lost. I walk past my bed and to the fireplace. There were already fresh logs put in for the evening. Helping him sit on the lounge and I make haste to start the fireplace. As I turn around, I fully take him in. It was a rarity to see him not in uniform and much less without any of his armor. His tunic was not the normal cream color but a dark color blue. Maybe his house color but I was not one for studies in such things and he wore black pants. His boots looked as if they were not tied or had loosen. Trailing back up to his face, his hair had mostly fallen out of his hair tie. There were some strains stuck to his forehead from sweat like he was working out or running at some point before coming to me.

He is staring at the fire as if the flames were dancing for his entertainment. I walk up to him and reach for his hair tie. Touching his hair triggered something. He snatches my wrist and met my gaze. Whatever he saw in my eyes, made his softened his already dark gaze and he lets go of my wrist. The warmth of his touch was replaced with the cold, paining me.

I took out his tie and let his hair fall, flowing around him like a waterfall. I run my fingers through hair, allowing my hands to trail down his neck. I watch him shudder. Carefully tuck my knees under me as I kneel in front of him. I could not bring myself to look at his face, which was probably just cold and distant. Unlacing his boots and taking them off. They were soaked. He must have been in the town's bar and walked this way here. His clothes look dry but his boots showed the evidence. If he was out there he would need to drink something to chase off any potential cold. He was in no position to leave and ask the kitchen staff or get it himself. So I stand up.

"I am going to get you some coffee." I look to the dark window that flashes with lightning outside and the sounds of the pitter patter rain intensifies. "It is last thing you need at this hour but it will help the whiskey and chase a cold away." I turn to leave his side. I was able to take a step but he stops me.

Grabbing my wrist and pulling me down. I fall into his lap. The sudden fall causes a gasp to escape my lips. He buries his head into my chest and pulled me in by wrapping his hands around my waist.

"I know it is indecent. I know people will talk but they already are. Please just stay. Stay here with me." His voice broke in vulnerability that completely shatters my heart.

I wrap my arms around Val, cradling his head against me and musing his hair. "Whatever you desire." I said the words that seems to have start it all. The words which were spoken just for her turns for him too. When it happens I could not pin-point it but I don't think I was ready to accept either. But I meant those three little words for Valin just as much as when I said them to Arabella.

The sounds of the crackling fireplaces, rain and our breaths filled the room. I felt the urge to place a tender kiss on the top of his head and the comfort of his arms was all too easy but not what he needed.

"At least let me ring someone to bring it."

"Just," he takes a deep breath. "Stay right here. Just like this. If you leave I feel I might fall apart." He whispers the last as if it was a secret. One he might forget what he said in the morning. His breathing seems to be deepening, his muscles relax and I think he might be falling asleep.

"I know, it seems comfy in this lounge now to sleep but I promise you will regret it in the morning." I pry his arms and stand helping him back onto his feet. I lead him to the bed but the bath caught my eyes. If he was not going to warm up with a drink some warm water would help. I walked past the bed and to the tub. It was already filled halfway with water that had turned warm.

"Okay before bed, at least a warm bath. No need to have the chilly down to the bones after the false warmth of the whiskey gives." He looks at me with suspicion almost like he was shy. "Don't worry I have seen it all helping in the infirmaries." I assure him and help him peel off his shirt. I have to go to the tips of my toes to get it completely off. His chest was not bare but it wasn't completely covered in hair either. A decent amount on his chest that trails to his abs but then stops. I glide my hands over them and to where the thin trail picks back up just under his belly button. I could feel his eyes on me but he never stopped me and his breathing continued to be deep and slow.

The lace of his trouser was already untied but I loosen them and help him out of them. I stand back up and met his gaze. The look of confusion and study was burning into me. "Why?" he asks. There could have been many why's. Why help him? Why be kind? Why did I do what I did? *But.*

"I don't know." the words flew out barely audible. The sounds of the words barely even sounded like my voice at all. I help him in the tub and ran to the draw string, pulling it twice. I keep an eye on him from the door and waited for the maid to come.

I hear the soft knock and I crack the door open. I block what I did open with my body. "I know I am asking for a lot. I know the maids gossip and know every secret thing going on in the castle but I need your discretion and help, please." Her eyes soften and she reaches out to take my hand.

"Whatever you need, your grace." she said. Whether she meant it or not I had placed my faith in her. I open the door more to show Valin was here.

"I need another basin full of hot water to warm the tub and

a pitcher of water with a glass. Maybe some mint in it to ease the stomach."

She nods with wide eyes and gave a quick curtsy before leaving. I wait by the door waiting to hear her returning footsteps. When I hear them I open the door for her. She brings the basin first. I could see the steam rising off the water. I grab one side to help carry it.

"Let me help." I insist before she could get her protest out. We walk to the end of the tub and pour it slowly. She hurries out for the pitcher. I hear the soft click of the door closing as I grab a wash rag.

I dip it in the water and move it around, leveling the water temperature. The warmth of the water enveloping my hand. Valin reaches out for the wash rag, catching my attention. Both of us holding it, neither one tugging for it. His eyes hold mine like he was searching for something but neither one said a word.

The small squeak of the door opening causes me to jump leaving the rag in his hands, alone. The maid had placed the pitcher of water with three mint leaves floating on top on my nightstand along with two empty glasses.

"Is there anything else you need, your grace?" She asks in a timid voice. She glances back and forth to Valin and me.

"No you are dismissed, thank you." I said. I watch her open and close her mouth before she looks at me over quickly.

"You are not in your evening gown. Would you like assistance?" She stops as I raise my hands.

"I can take care of myself tonight. Please do remember what I requested though, discretion. If someone asks you please avoid Valin's name on your lips." She nods at my words, giving a small bow before leaving the room. I kept my back turned from Valin, trying to give as much privacy as this chamber gave.

I walk to the nightstand, pouring him a glass of water. Watching a leaf fall into the glass. All the while I could hear the water moving around. The scrubbing of his skin, suds popping and the sloshing of water. I could not just stand at the nightstand so I started moving the decorative pillows to the lounge and pulling the duvet down. I paused at the sounds of him getting out of the water. I could hear him drying off and what sounded like the tuck of his towel. I turn around when I think he is covered.

"I can call the maid back to get you clean clothes. It slipped my mind to tell her." His hair was still dripping. His chest bare and the towel barely covering his waist. His feet took the couple steps that separated us and closed the distance between us. I look back at his face. He looks hauntingly beautiful. My breathing became shallow, the rise of my chest brushing and meeting his chest. His head hovering over my face, droplets falling from the tips of his hair onto my skin. I couldn't help but shiver as they rolled along. Thoughts of his fingertips bring that sensation of the water droplets. As much as I wanted and desired him, I would not push him. He wraps his arm around my waist, pulling me in and cupping my neck.

His eyes stare at my lips, I felt as if I could not breathe right. The anticipation of a kiss. He starts to meet my lips with his and I know if I meet them again I would not want to stop. I cover his mouth with my hands. His brows furrowed in confusion.

"You are still intoxicated and don't really want this. You are hurt, angry and not thinking clearly." I said and moving my hands.

"I am angry. Angry, I let her down. Angry, I started looking at you in the first place. Angry, my feelings for you are there. I have never been able to sway from her before. I am angry that I enjoyed it even though while I was with you enjoying it, she got taken. Angry that even if I wanted to blame you, I can't." He closes his eyes and leans his forehead against mine. "I wanted so much to drink my shame away and still found myself walking to you for help as I was trying to drown myself. I don't know how to be without her, my duty but I don't want to be without you either. And somehow I feel like I lost all three."

"We will find her." I cup his face and held his gaze. "We can leave in the morning, together." I said the last would with a strong feeling that made my heart swell.

"They will talk. I was ordered to stand down in my station."

"They may talk but no one notices me. I won't be missed at first. We have maybe three days tops before anyone notices I am gone." I chuckled halfheartedly trying to lighten his mood.

"I notice you, Aerilyn." He growls out my name before he crashes his lips to mine. His hand on my neck slides into my hair and he tangles his fingers into it. The sensation of him tucking my head back slightly causes me to moan against his lips. Parting my lips briefly, my tongue meet his. The grip of his hand on my waist tightens as he groans in desperation.

It was entirely to hot, I break away breathless. Fanatically pulling and struggling with the corset ties behind me. He makes hot trails of kisses down my neck and growls as he tries to pull it apart. Failing, he flips me around and I brace my hands on the bed to keep from falling.

"I dislike these things." He declares as he quickly opens the corset and flings it somewhere in the room. "But I like this view." he says as rips open the back of my dress.

Aerilyn: Caught in Feelings

The cold air pricking my skin. I felt his hands trail down my spine with the slightest touch, widening the torn fabric as it fell. I turn to met his lips with desperation. Kicking the fabric pooling at my feet.

He leans into me and grips my hips as if I was going to run from him. Pain and pleasure mixing with his hold on me. I can't help but moan as he pushes me onto the bed. I was fully ready to feel his body over mine. Feel him part my legs with his knee as he made himself comfortable as I willing give myself to him, but there was a pause.

I prob myself on my elbows to see him knelt before me. His head above my knees. My breath caught at the sight of him. The look of desire was rippling out of his darken eyes. He ran his finger tips down from the top of my stockings to the boot. I open my legs for him in anticipation.

"You did not think I would fuck you with out giving you the treatment you deserve, did you?" In a fluid motion he takes my boots off. "To just fuck you while I have yet to completely undress you? Who have you played with, Little Temptress?" He glides his hands down with my stockings. Placing a kiss on the inside of my thighs. He gives a devilish smile as he calls me that name. Before I could find the words to articulate a response, I watch him grip my waist and pull me to the edge of the bed and spreading my legs wide open.

Completely exposed, I feel sensations as the air kisses my hard nipples. Also the air kissing me below. A slow torturous hand snakes along my thigh towards it. I through my head back unable to take my own bodies response to my hips bucking to meet his hand.

"Please," I plea but barely able to get the word out. My chest heaves trying to catch my breath but it is hard as my heart feels like a hummingbird in the middle of summer. He hums against my inner thigh. Dragging his lips back up to me.

I could not help but moan while he slides into me. It was slow and torturous at first. It felt as though he was savoring the moment until neither of couldn't take it any long. The deny of something we both wanted for so long.

He set the pace as I demand for more. I wanted it all, every last drop of carnal desires that made no promises for tomorrow. For the first time, I felt I was souring to the sky.

He ravage my neck with kisses and bites that had me touching the clouds. I was someone flying that threaten to fall. I was not afraid of the fall.

I hold on to him, wrapping my legs and arms around him. He grips my waist tighter. I welcome for any marks that would remind me of this moment for days to come. To tell me that it was real.

I cry out in delight, feeling the rush of falling straight into the crashing waves of euphoria. There came the silence the realization of what we did. Neither on regretting but not wanting to see if the other did.

He peppers kisses along my neck and we made our way onto the pillows finally. He holds me tightly as I hold him. No words, just two people not ready to crumple the walls we both spent our lives building. I listen to the thrumming of his heart and the deep breathing. I want to memorize it. To always have that to hold dear.

King: The Seer

She was gone. It was not an almost attempt, but that damn creature got her this time. I knew I should have said no to Valin's request days ago, but it seemed to be a solid plan. A moment of weakness for a father to please his daughter.

If I could take it all back, I would. Her safety is more important than her happiness. I hold those papers in my hand as everyone was in my chambers. Something dark was coming. There is war brewing, and this is just one of the many things that will happen. The first steps, if you will. All I had to do was protect her. All I had to do was make sure he did not take her.

Maybe it could be stopped. It was before when we stopped this thing from taking her last time. Does that mean war is coming? Obviously, the other kingdoms feel it, too. I mean, that was the whole reason Sir Keiran came in the first place. Maybe allegiance to what was to come.

I see a handful of guards next in line after Valin standing around me, waiting. Valin, damn idiot. He knew what was at stake. I will deal with him later. I had no patience to look at his idiotic face. If she is brought back safely, I might feel better and forgive him, but there are too many *ifs* right now.

"I want scouts out right now and another set sent in the morning. Understand?" I know I sound rough, but I don't care. I want my daughter safe. There was a string of 'Yes, your majesty' before they filter out.

I sit on my throne and find no strength to sit up. Looking like a weak king, but I had no care to fix that. I was human to with human emotions. I could not be strong all the time like everyone expected me to.

I hold the papers that I hold and carry everywhere. They were old things. Folded, yellow with age and rough around the edges.

They were some of the last things my wife, my queen, wrote. Very few knew she was a seer. One that was blessed by the gods or cursed. One to know what is going to happen with little or no direction to stop it. I thought it was a good thing until the day our daughter was born.

She was plagued with visions of wars that were coming. One that no man has seen before. Our daughter kidnapped by a creature who thought of himself as a god. One that should have died long ago.

I looked at the words over and over. Nothing told me how to get her back. I could not stop, almost like it was fate. *Was it fate?*

It was hard to deny with all the evidence pointing towards it.

Arabella: Captured

My eyes are closed, and they feel so heavy, I try to move, but the arms behind my back wouldn't budge as if I had been restrained. It was so cold and the rocky floor underneath my bottom was undesirable.

Slowly, I muster enough strength to open my eyes. I look around and see we are in a dark cave there were dripping water in certain parts. The stone floor felt cold to the touch. I look over my shoulder and see a rope tied around my wrists. I try to pull them apart but they had been tied too tight.

"Nice to see you're finally awake, princess. How are you feeling?" a voice said. It was a raspier voice, deeper than Val's.

I look up and see a figure of what seems to be a man. The man is tall. He looks to be six feet tall. He is wearing a long black cloak; the hood hiding most of his face.

"Who are you?" I ask my body shivering, not knowing if it was from the cold or fear, or both.

"That is not important right now," he replies simply as his back leans against the wall.

To Be Damned

We stay silent. The only sound that I could make out is the rain outside. I stare at him, trying to see any sign of what he looks like. The hood was good at hiding how he looks.

As if he could feel my stare on him, he tilts his head to look at me. I frown, getting a glimpse of one of his eyes. It is an amber color and looks as if they were glowing.

"Why did you take me?" I ask trying to get some answer from him.

"You will find out soon enough when the witch gets here." I look at him as if he had two heads.

"Witch?" I question "are you crazy!?"

"You have her eyes, you know," he responds. His voice was now teasing. I look at him, my face frowning in confusion.

"Her eyes? You knew the queen?" I ask, curiosity now filling me. If I could at least get him talking to me, maybe I could convince him to let me go.

"No. There was a woman a long time ago. Everyone looked up to her. She was the light of this town. She had so much life, but she was taken from this world." he explains, he looks out towards the entrance to the cave, almost as if he was expecting her to come in through there.

"And what has she got to do with me?"

"She died a long time ago. The world isn't always so kind. Sometimes humans are more of monsters than actual monsters," he explains, still looking at the entrance of the cave. I try thinking about his words. He speaks as if he's witnessed monsters before.

"So your love died… what does that have to do with me?" I ask him, feeling anxious. He turns back to me, his face still abstracted by his hood.

"Have you ever seen things that were unexplainable? Like a

glimpse of yourself somewhere else in time."

"No, I don't think" I stop myself and think. I remember the dream and frown wondering if that is what he meant. "I saw myself in your arms in a dream. I was dead. Is that what you mean?"

"Yes. When she died, I had such a hatred for this town. I wanted to burn it to the ground, but every time I would try, I couldn't. It was as if her ghost was haunting me, telling me not to do it. I prayed to the bastard gods to bring her back to me, that I would give anything for her again. After sometime I realize the gods had turned their backs, that fate had predestined things in motion. That I just need to wait out my time to see her soul filtered back into this forsaken world." He said the story was so sad it must have hurt him to have lost her.

"And what do you plan once her soul filters back? You had obviously taken me for a reason. Why now?"

"Oh, princess, you are not the brightest, are you? No matter, you are her soul. You and her are one and the same." My face reddens when he jokes about my intellect. I glare at him.

"You are saying that me and this woman are one soul?" I huff a laugh. "You really are crazy! Magic isn't real. It's all fiction"

"You can believe what you want." He says and suddenly I feel lightheaded from this news.

"Listen, my guards will be on their way to rescue me. Why don't we save an unnecessary fight and go on our separate ways"

"Guards? Like the one that was in the tent in the arms of another woman? Weren't you two supposed to marry? Low standards princess," he teases. I grimace at him talking about Val he didn't understand our.... Circumstance.

"And if your plans go accordingly? You get your love back? What happens to my soul? You said we were one and the same and I certainly wouldn't love a man who would kidnap me"

"Oh, you poor sheltered child, you have been protected from the secrets of this world. You truly don't know the darkness, do you?" He teases again, and I keep my mouth shut. "I need to go out, so I need you to sleep Princess," he stands up, grabbing a cloth that I was sure had that stuff on it from last time. I shake my head no and try to shuffle away.

"No, please don't," I beg. He was now in front of me with the cloth.

"I'll be back soon, sleep tight" and that was the last thing I heard before the cloth was on me and everything went dark.

Aerilyn: Focus

We slip out of the castle before the sun could spot us. Valin had seen tracks that led to the mountains before the rain and his title stripping. I hoped the rain had not washed them all away last night.

We walk and see the fading footprints that led to the mountains and into deeper into the woods. We walk with each other, mostly in silence. Neither one daring to speak what was shared between us. An unspoken understanding that nothing could come of it. Valin knew what was to come. He knew Keiran was courting me. He also wanted the princess's hand.

To stay would mean I would share their bed. Maybe their hearts, but never be an equal to them.

The deeper we travel into the woods, I feel my senses were coming alive. There was something that sang to my heart. Enticing me to follow this invisible pull. I found I was no longer looking for the footstep, but I must have been going the right way because Valin was not correcting me. I was now ahead of him by a few paces and the lightness I felt was unlike anything I had felt before.

"Aerilyn?" His voice was like a melody sung out of tune as I was dancing towards something anew.

"Yes," I did not miss a step as we head towards the heart of this beat.

"You seem off. Are you okay?"

"Yes," He follows me after that, not saying anything.

After hours of chasing this feeling, I stumble on an entrance of a cave. Valin grabs my arm and pulls me behind him.

"Stay behind me," He orders. His face was full of determination, but his stance was cautious about me this close to danger.

I felt no urgency, no fear of this. I knew I should be scared, but something in my veins flowed. For the first time, I felt I was where I belonged. I shove down those feelings the best I could and follow silently behind Valin.

Valin: Blood of Blood

I follow Aerilyn to the cave. She was going the right way where the footsteps lead us, but something was off in her presence. Like she was drunk without having a drop today. I pull her behind me. She really was about to walk in a dark cave without a care about what may be in there.

With soft footing, I take my time entering. I listen for any noises but only hearing the dripping somewhere deep. The light quickly disappearing the deeper we made it in, but my eyes were able to adjust to the differences.

I feel Aerilyn tug on my sleeve. I turn and look at her. Her amber eyes now glowing like a fire. She looks as if she wanted to say something but did not say.

"What?"

"I don't know. I feel like. Just be careful." There is a worried look. She looks like she wanted to say more, but what I was not sure. I turn and continue on. There was a growing sound of cracking fire and a faint glow in the deep.

I slow my step and can hear a deep voice talking to a woman.

It was not the princess' voice though. It was someone I could not realize the tone alone. The words were coming to me clearer as we got closer.

"I thought you said you would be ready, *witch*." This stranger's voice sneer with so much disdain.

"You put words in my mouth. Again. I said I would be ready at the full moon. It is not a full moon till the sun lays down and allows the moon to rise tonight." Her words come out like wisp and breathless. Something so soft to her tone. It is something that could be easily looked over as a sweet elderly woman.

I round a curve and hug the wall. Using the shadows to cast some cover. I turn to Aerilyn and see the same look in her eyes, but something more is added. Wonder and curiosity. Like a moth to a flame. I grab her arm and pull her in. Snapping her attention as I whisper in her ear.

"Go, leave and bring people back." There is a look of shock when I let go of her arm.

"No." She mouths the worlds in defiance. I pull her back in.

"Do it. There are two of them that have her." I throw her arm a bit to get her out of here. She stumbles with it but turned to leave.

A part of me felt I could breathe easier. It would have been hard to focus if I had to fight one of them. There was more than one, if not more. There could have been more in there, and I have no way of knowing.

I listen and hear the male shh the woman.

"I think there is someone else here." The male whispers.

"Figure out your things. Come get me later tonight." The woman had said, and I feel a breeze like a strong wind coming from within. I grip the hilt of the sword and brace before I come around the bend.

Valin: Blood of Blood

I made a quick scan of the area. There was no woman but a fire that was in the middle of the area. The princess tied up and her eyes closed along the cave wall. I knew I heard a male's voice before I made it in here.

I see shadows dancing in the corner of my vision. Turning around quickly, I raise my sword just in time as the shadow figure's hand came down in a claw. I expect to see blood as the very least, even more so, his hand.

Before he moves it back, I notice the scales. It looks like snake scales peppered his skin on his arm, with his hand elongated into talons. His arm starts to slide up the blade and I look to see his face. He looks to be human, but his eyes look familiar.

He smiles his taunt before he starts his dance is swings. The quick attacks making it hard to block but too fast to put any power behind it.

I was on complete defense, not able to make any attacks of my own. His amber eyes being wilder with each swing.

"Are you getting tired, princeling?" His sinster voice spoke the words with ease, like he wasn't even close to being tired from his quick attacks.

"I don't know who you think I am, but I am no prince."

There is a quick swipe from his right claws that I block. I feel the sting as I feel his left claw came in and pierce my armour. He removes the claw and slowly licks the blood off it.

"I know." He said, his eyes closed while he was licking his claw.

I step in with my sword and bring it down to his neck. He moves too fast for me to follow. There is a sharp pain causing me to drop my sword. He grips me by the throat and slams me into the wall behind me. Knocking all the air out of my lungs.

"Did you really think you could beat me?" His hand starts to tighten around my neck.

"Do you realize who I am? How old I am?" Tighter, Tighter. The pressure of his hand was becoming increasingly hard to breathe. I hold on to his forearm. It felt like an iron bar.

"I was around when the gods walked this world. I was one with them!" My vision was starting to spot. Out of desperation, I reach for his eyes. I just need him to loosen his hold for a moment. I felt a sickening feeling as struck out for his eyes.

He releases his hold slightly, giving me air, and I swiftly grip his forearm and pulling it from my neck. Driving my knee up into his gut. I hear his air get knocked out of him as he doubles over. I try to knock him out by bringing my elbow up and smashing it as hard as I could to the back of his head.

The act alone has me staggering back. I expect him to fall to the ground, but to my horror, he rubs the back of his head and stood back up. I see movement to where Arabella was and snap my attention for a split second.

I see Aerilyn with a dagger cutting Arabella free. And I felt a small amount of relief. I did not think I would win against this thing, but I could try to distract him long enough with them running out.

That moment of distraction costing me as I get punched in the gut. I instinctively block my face as I anticipate the next blow to there. I stumble back and side step so his back was to what Aerilyn was doing.

Like clockwork, he follows me. We start our new dance of swing and dodging. I dodge one of his swings and close the distance. Sweeping my leg from under him, I move to get behind him. Kicking the back of his knee.

Before he completely falls, I wrap my arm around his neck and lock it with my other. I wanted to see if they got out, but

Valin: Blood of Blood

I had to use all my strength to hold him in place. He tries to throw me off, but I tighten my hold.

I feel his clawed hands grip my forearm and his body starts to relax back. I knew what he was about to do. He was going to try to throw me over him, but I press the hand behind his head. Taking his advantage away.

I hear an unearthly growl emanate from his chest and his body getting bigger. The scales from his arms now showing up on his neck. The once human looking skin around his neck looking more like a dragon.

But that was not possible. They were not real. Nothing but a story in books. Stories to scare children to stay out of the woods.

His neck expanding, with one move he had thrown me off. The back of my head snapping and hitting the wall behind me. Before I could clear my vision, he presses his foot on my chest. The pressure alone making it hard to breathe and forces all the air out my lungs.

Out of nowhere, I see Aerilyn jumping on his back. He stubbed his foot that was on me. He reaches behind him and I try to move, but it happened fast to react.

He grabs Aerilyn. He had a hold of her cloak. She shakes it off, snaking around him, and drives the dagger into his chest. There is a look of surprise as he sees her face. The glow of his eyes starting to dim. He starts to raise his hand and touches her face. She jerks her hand, twisting the dagger.

The blood starting to come out of his mouth as he coughs. He never moves his hand. Never tried to hurt her. The look of shock and sorrow painted on his face.

"Blood of blood," he chokes out before falling on his knees. She pulls the dagger, and he falls on his face with a sickening thud.

I lean my back to the cave walls and slide down to sit. I was so tired. My muscles screaming and I was so sore. The princess comes running from the side of me. Falling into me.

Cupping my face, she looks me over, checking to see if I had any serious injuries. One she sees that I will live, she rests her forehead on mine.

"You're okay," *Kiss, kiss, kiss.* "I'm so sorry. This is all my fault. I saw you both together." *Kiss, kiss, kiss.* "You have to know, both of you" She looks back at Aerilyn who was staring at the bloody, covered dagger and back to me. "I want to be with you both. I love you both." She places a kiss not on my face, but on my lips.

I break the kiss and stand up, holding her close to me.

"I love you too, but let's get out of here." Aerilyn looks up at us. The burning look was now gone. She looked like she had lost something.

"Yes, please." Aerilyn whispers, dropping the dagger next to the strangers body and walking out of the cave. I pick the princess up and carry her home.

Aerilyn: I wanted you both

Valin held on to Arabella, carrying her all the way back to the castle. There was a few times she in complain that she could walk but Valin did not humor her.

When we get back to the castle, everyone comes in with deep relief to see her. The King came in a rush, kissing her forehead but allowing Valin to carry her in the rest of the way. I could see my own father somewhere in the mix. His eyes were like dagger but I pretend not to see them. I was a mess, and I wanted to bathe. The same for the princess and Valin, I was sure.

There is things that happened today that I was not sure I was ready to be wrapped around. Things that I was not sure I wanted to know was true. I wanted to bury those memories and move on.

I split off from Valin and Arabella to make my way to my room. Walking in, Keiran sat on my bed. I meet his eyes and close the door.

"You are back safe." His words were just trying to fill the silence and avoid the question that was eating at him. I could see it in his eyes. He wanted to know.

"Nothing happened. I just wanted to make sure they got home safe. I am really tired. Can we talk later?" He closes the distance between us and picks up my hand. Placing a soft kiss on top.

"Of course,"

After he left, I bathe and try to sleep. I toss and turn. I had this feeling I was about to miss something. The princess' words swam in my head. *I wanted you both.*

The words dance around my head like butterfly not able to sit in the windstorm. Something I want to give her but never be able to have her keep. I could not even bring myself to tell her about my courtship with Keiran. That I will be leaving this island and would not have the heart to write to her in my own shame.

It will go back to the way it was after my mother died. She would continue on and I would be a fleeting memory to her. Someone she once desired, someone to be damned for any pleasures of this world. It would be greedy for me to want more, but I do.

She would be fine with her knight in shining armor. Forever the man who saved her from the big dragon. The dragon which made himself look man for the most part. Something I hope I one day can forget. His eyes looking at me like I was someone he knew. I will work on forgetting his words, eyes and his blood that stained my hands. Just as she might forget me. A fond memory, maybe.

Arabella: The Aftermath

I lay in bed with my eyes closed, praying for sleep to take me away. It never does. It felt like my brain was a mass of a whirlwind of emotions. My chest felt tighter than usual. I almost feel as if I couldn't breathe.

Eventually, I sit up and get out of the bed. I stand and walk around the room, trying to find anything to help entertain my brain enough for me to get to sleep. A knock at the door stops me in my tracks. I freeze, a feeling of fear hitting me all over again.

"Princess? Are you awake?" I hear Valin's voice on the other side of the door. I sigh with relief. Taking a deep breath to calm down, I turn to face the door, my hands moving in front of me clasped together.

"Come in," I say loud enough for him to hear. He slowly opens the door and walks in, shutting the door behind him. He bows and then looks at me.

"Couldn't sleep?" He asks, looking at my eyes. They were probably sporting dark circles underneath them. I clear my throat.

"I got lost in my books is all, I didn't realize how late it was" I lie, his face shows that he didn't believe me but he didn't bring it up again.

"If you're sure, I talked with your father and got his permission for the marriage," He tells me and I frown, confused.

"But you won the tournament? Why wouldn't you have his permission?" I ask and watch as he rubs his hand over his face and then looks at me.

"Because I let you down on your name day. He ordered me to keep you safe, and I didn't. I thought he might have called it off, but he didn't," He replies and I sigh, moving closer to him. I stand on my tiptoes and place a soft kiss on his cheek.

"As much as you blame yourself for what happened, I am at fault too," I say and he opens his mouth to argue but I put a finger to his lips "I walked away from the guards, yes to look for you but I did. I was the one who cried to you to leave the castle walls, and maybe I was naïve to think I would be safe. I don't think I'll ever be safe because of my title. But in a few days we will be married and all of this will just be a distant nightmare. So go back to your room and rest. I'm sure Owen will keep me company if need be." He sighs and nods.

He looks down at my arms and looks at the bruises on my wrists from where the ropes were tied. He lifts my arms up to his mouth, and he kisses both wrists softly. The feel of his lips on me caught me by surprise at first, for a Knight that was so worried about touching me because of consequences he was doing a good job of it now. He is gentle and soft, moving his mouth carefully as if I would disappear from him.

"I'm here Valin, because of you and because of Aerilyn." I feel tears in my eyes and the illusion I had of being okay was slowly dissipating. The tear falls quick, so quick I couldn't blink it away. I look down quickly, praying that he didn't see the tear, but I should have known that he would notice. His index finger moves underneath my chin and pushes my chin up to look at him.

"What's the matter Princess? And the truth this time," He orders, causing me to smile sadly at him.

"You're giving me orders now?" I joke trying to find some light in this situation.

"Only when it comes to your well being" His hand moves up to my cheek and rubs away the line of water the tear had left behind, my body shakes slightly and I wasn't sure if it was out of fear or the feel of his hand on me after the night we shared.

"What if he comes back and succeeds next time? If I remember that past that he talked about, and I change and become a person I don't like. What if next time he comes he will take me somewhere and you won't be able to find me?" I asked multiple questions, and the tears were rushing down my cheeks, matching the rain outside pattering against the window. He stays quiet for a moment and then pulls me into his embrace.

"That is a lot what if's. It's about what happens now that matters. What happened won't just go away and you will always have the memories of it all. But the strength you have will help you get through it. You are the heart of these people." His words made my heart flutter and I rest my forehead on his chest, breathing in his scent.

"And you will be there by my side won't you Val, you'll always be there" I say more than a statement then a question, I look up and see a smile on his face, a true and real smile that I haven't seen from him before.

"Try to stop me Princess," He replies and I slap my hand on his chest playfully .

"Arabella, when we are alone, you stubborn man." I remind him, and he chuckles.

"Let's get you to bed Princess" He leads me to the bed holding out the covers, I climb in and he pulls them over me tucking me in. He crouches down as I rest my head on the pillow. I close my eyes slowly feeling the heaviness of my lids. His hand moves to mine and gives it a comforting squeeze.

"Goodnight Val," I say tiredly and snuggle into the pillow. I hear his heavy footsteps moving to the door.

"Sleep tight, Arabella" was the last thing I heard before the door shut. I smile softly at him, finally saying my name. Not long after sleep took me and I went into a deep dreamless sleep.

Arabella: A Royal wedding

The nerves were kicking in like bricks. I stare out of the window, watching many people moving around different items, there are thousands of flower pots being moved around, people are lighting lanterns and resting them on the floor as a lit up entry way to the palace. I would enter through there tomorrow in a wedding dress, I wipe the sweat that gathers on my hands from nerves onto the simple dress I was wearing.

As much as this is all I have ever wanted I couldn't help but feel nervous, thousands of eyes will be watching me tomorrow, I kept having nightmares of me falling over or vomiting on a random person who would be there just to witness the wedding.

"You're not having second thoughts are you princess" I hear behind me causing me to jump I turn around and see Val shutting the door behind him. He walked further into the room and bowed.

"I did knock but you mustn't have heard, are you okay?" He

asks and I nod.

"I'm fine I just, worry about making a mistake tomorrow" I confess moving closer to him. He smiles at me and holds my left hand pulling it between us as we both look down to the ring he had chosen for me.

"Tomorrow we will be married" he observed staring at the ring. I couldn't pin his emotions whether he was nervous or excited or scared or happy, he was always the one person I could never figure out what he was feeling.

"You know it's not too late to run if that's what you want to do" I joke looking up at him, he smiled and looked down to me.

"I would never run from you princess" he whispers, then as he stared at me something in his eyes flash, a sense of guilt. I squeeze the hand that is holding mine, I brought it up to my lips and kiss his hand the surprise in his face made me smile.

"Val, I can still see the guilt in your eyes, what happened it wasn't your fault. If anything it was mine, I had no sense of danger I thought you were all being over protective, I never really understood the world. So please, no more guilt I'm okay, we are okay"

"I should've been there to stop it" he carries on but I shook my head placing my finger tips on his lips to quiet him.

"We do not talk about it anymore, I'm here and so are you, tomorrow I will marry you and you will become my prince. Everything is good, okay?" I reply to him and he nods and kisses the fingers that were lay on his lips.

"Are you 100% sure this is what you want Valin?" I ask again and he grins pulling away from me and goes down to his knee, he holds my hand gently as if I were made of glass.

"Princess Arabella, marrying you tomorrow will be the

Arabella: A Royal wedding

greatest honor I could ever be granted in life. I grin looking down at him the butterflies in my stomach were overwhelming, I bite my lip looking down.

"Well good, and might I say Sir Valin I do rather like see you on your knees for me." I blush and grin backing away two steps he grins standing up and bows again.

"Tomorrow Princess" He says and I nod. He smiles turning around and walking out of the room shutting the door as he leaves.

"Till tomorrow" I whisper to myself still looking at the door as if he were still there. I turn and lie in bed and close my eyes praying to whatever Gods are out there to bring all of the luck tomorrow.

***

I was awoken at the early hours of the morning with my maids coming into the room. They brought in food for me to eat, it was mostly porridge with different types of fruit I could add to it if that is what I wanted, I chose to add some strawberries as I ate my maids were gushing over the wedding dress they had chosen.

Once I had finish with the food, I clean in the wash room making sure to clean every part of my body. Once I step out a robe, I am instantly wrap around my body and a towel was wrapped around my hair.

They quickly drag me to the vanity where two maids towel dried my hair and style it and the other maid was putting makeup on my face. I was getting the feeling of being a rag doll to the maids, and as much as I wanted to think about the wedding they didn't give me much time with the hair pulling and different makeup products making it extra close to my eyes.

They finish styling my hair, they added volume to the back and kept it down and curly, they added small diamonds and tied them in different parts of the curls, My make up was simple but elegant with golds and browns, my lips were painted a pale pink, the maid rubbed scented oils on my neck and wrists. The dress was then brought out by two of the maids, it was gorgeous. It looks like a princess dress there were diamonds covering the bodice and a hooped skirt bottom.

I was helped into the underskirt that would help give the bottom of my dress more volume. Then they help me climb into the dress, they pulled it up and I held the chest part of the dress to me while they buttoned the bottom half and then tied the string at the top where the bodice was.

A maid brought a beautiful lacy veil, she walks over clipping it into the top of my hair. Half of the veil flows down the back and the the other half covers my face.

"I don't wish to have my face covered." I say not liking the feel of me being hidden.

"Well princess it is tradition to have your face covered until the future prince sees you in the ceremony." the maid explains and I roll my eyes, tradition sucks. I move the front part of the veil out of my face and over my hair for now. I look into the floor length mirror, I didn't recognize the woman looking back at me. For once I felt and looked like a elegant princess, I smile softly feeling some confidence.

A knock at the door startles me I turn around frowning wondering who could be knocking on a day like today. A maid opens the door revealing Aerilyn wearing a beautiful dress. It was a floor length olive green dress. The elegant dress that falls

Arabella: A Royal wedding

on her figure, off her shoulders with intricate details of vines and roses. I smile widely then look towards all of the maids in the room.

"Please give us some privacy." I order and they quickly nod and rush out of the room shutting the door behind them. I smile at her and she smiles back we rush towards each other and hug each other tightly.

"You look beautiful." I tell her breathing her in.

"Me? Look at you, you look breathtaking." Aerilyn replies and I grin pulling back, something looked different in her eyes I frown.

"Are you sure you are okay with this, I want you to be happy too." I say and she smiles shaking her head.

"I am happy I promise." she says and walks up to me and kisses my cheek softly. "Thank you" she carries on and I frown confused.

"For what?" I ask and she shakes her head.

"You'll figure it out one day Arabella. Now lets get you married"

"Okay." I link my arm in hers and I smile at her "I love you Aerilyn, please never change who you are" She looks away from a moment as if she was composing herself, something was definitely off I would have to ask her about it after the wedding.

"As you wish." she simply said as she lead us out of the castle and into the gardens where Val would be waiting.

Once we got to the front of the castle I smile at my father who was waiting for me, Aerilyn moved my arm to my father and gives me a final smile before she went to sit down with everyone else, I swore I saw water fill her eyes but I couldn't have been sure.

To Be Damned

"Ready?" my father asks and I nod feeling like I could vomit any moment. He grabs the veil but I place my hand on his to stop him, he pauses.

"Sometimes traditions really should be broken." I grin at him and he nods a grin on his face.

"As you wish sunshine." He starts walking down the aisle that was full of wild flower petals, the same kind of wild flower that Valin had once gifted to me. The lanterns glows making everything look like a fairy tail.

Valin is waiting at the front in front of a priest he didn't turn to look which was another tradition, the man was not suppose to look until the bride was in front of them. My father kept leading me, each side of us was hundreds and hundreds of chairs full of people I didn't know I tried to smile at as many of them as I could.

We got to the front where Valin stood my father squeezed my hand gently and smiles.

"Who gives this woman away?" The priest asks

"I do." my father announces and Val finally turns to face me, he looked so handsome in his formal wear. My father moves my hand into Valins and kisses my cheek before he goes and sits in his chair. I take a deep breath and smile at Val, the nerves felt like they disappeared as if this was where I was meant to be.

I look up and see him mouth 'You look beautiful'. I blush and look to the priest unable to stop the grin on my face. The ceremony was awfully dull, the priest kept reciting verses from the ancient Gods but I couldn't pay attention to this as I had a gorgeous man in front of me.

"Do you Princess Arabella take Sir Valin to be your husband?" The Priest asks.

Arabella: A Royal wedding

"I do"

"And do you Sir Valin take Princess Arabella to be your wife?" He asks Valin

"I do" Valin grins making me grin back.

"By the power invested in me I now pronounce you man and wife, you may kiss the bride" Instantly Val's lips were on mine, it was a soft but sweet kiss. I grin into the kiss and as much as I wanted to stay kissing him I don't think it would be proper to the guests so we pull back and face everyone watching.

***

The party was well underway. Me and Val had to greet many guests. It was getting tiring. Who could remember these people's names?

"You sure you didn't make a mistake marrying me? This is so tiring. My feet hurt," I groaned, watching the guests dance to the songs played by violinists.

"I'll make sure to rub your feet later Princess," Val smiles and then holds his arm out to me to dance. I take it and he leads me to the dance floor. People move out of the way for us and give us a wide birth. We slowly dance to the music, our bodies close together. We didn't speak, but we enjoy the closeness. I rest the side of my head on his chest as we sway.

As much as I was having fun and enjoying this party, I was exhausted. It was always customary for the bride and groom to be the last ones to leave their wedding, but we decided to break tradition. I look at Val and his eyes were on me, raising my eyebrow at him questioningly, wondering if he had stopped looking at me at all today.

"I would like to go back to my room now," I say to him, placing

To Be Damned

a hand on his. My satin glove covered it, but I could still feel the warmth of his hand on mine.

"Are you sure? There is probably a chance your father may send guards to find us and bring us back." I laugh at his wariness.

Looking over to where my father was, he was over towards a painting was of my mother. Something he wanted was for her to be in this room, to feel like she was here. He placed his hand on it and I could see a tear fall down his cheek, which he quickly wiped away before anybody else could notice.

"I think we will be okay, he is occupied right now," I smile and drag Valin with me towards my room.

The halls were quiet. The only noise coming is from our footsteps. We didn't speak; we walk hand in hand as equals. I didn't look at what guards followed us. I didn't care anymore. Valin opens the door and waits for me to walk in before him, always a gentleman. I walk into the middle of the room and look over my shoulder towards Valin. He shut the door and slowly walks towards me. Turning to face him, I smooth out the crease of the dress.

"Would you like me to ask for your maids to help you change?" He asks, *was he nervous? Or was I imagining it?*

"No, it is fine. Would you help me untie my corset? I will change myself," I say confidently and turn around so he could access the ribbons on the back of my dress. His finger tips caress my shoulder and I frown, tilting my head to the side so I could see his expression.

His stare was so intense and his fingertips felt like fire on my skin, he is still being cautious around me, as if he was still wondering if he was what I wanted my hand moves onto his and give it a little squeeze, a small sign of confirmation that I wanted him.

He releases a small breath, one I didn't know he was holding. He unties the ribbons at an exceptionally slow pace, as if he was taking his time with it to savor this moment. Once he finished untying the ties completely, I expected him to move away, but he didn't. He stays in the spot as if he was glued to it.

I turn to face him, my chest brushing against his. He was so close that I could feel his breath on my face. Taking the smallest step back so we weren't too close, I smile up at him.

"Thank you" my voice was barely a whisper, he nods slowly still not making any noise. The tension in the room was burning me alive.

I move my hand to take off my glove when his hand grabs onto my elbow, not roughly it was a soft touch. I pause and look up at him. He has a small smile on his face, one I would engrave into my memory.

"Let me," he says as his other hand moves to the tip of my fingers. Slowly, he pulls each finger of the glove off my hand, one by one. After he pulls off all the fingers, he removes the glove completely and places it on a lounge chair. He stares at my bare arm. I could see the movement of his neck as if he had gulped. He brings my hand up to his face and places a gentle kiss on my wrist. Although it was a small gesture, it caused my heart to beat so fast that I swore the pulse was visible through my skin.

He slowly drops my hand and moves to my other hand. Sure enough, he repeats what he had done to my other hand, removing each finger of the glove one by one agonizingly slow. And just like the last time he moves my hand to his lips and kisses my wrist again, an audible breath left my lips as he looks into my eyes.

To Be Damned

"I will wait here for you, Arabella. There is a robe in the bathroom," He said as he steps back, his hands going behind his back. Something he would have to break a habit of once king.

I nod at him and walk to the bathroom and shut the door behind me. Pulling the dress down and step out of it, leaving a big clump on the floor. I walk to the mirror and look at my reflection, the makeup still on my face almost perfectly still. My rag cloth was on the vanity in front of me. I soak it in water and rub it gently on my face to get everything of I scrunch my face at the now discolored rag and throw it into my wash basket. I grab the robe that was hanging on the back of the door, putting it on. The silk felt smooth against my. skin. Looking back to the mirror, I felt happy with my appearance and walk out into the bedroom where Val was lay in the lounge, looking towards the fire in front of him, the blaze burning had him deep in thought as if the flames were telling him a secret.

Smiling at him, I sit down next to him, my feet curled underneath me and my body facing him.

"How are you feeling?" I ask, and he smiles at me, causing my heart to flutter.

"I'm good, how are you?" he asks back and I nod at him, my lips grinning from ear to ear. We didn't say anything after that, we just stare at each other as if our eyes were doing the talking. I was finally ready to make the first move to lean forward and join our lips, praying it would be everything I wanted it to be and more. Just as I was about to move to him I hear a knock on the door, turning towards it confused wondering who would disturb a bride and groom on their wedding night.

"Come in" I shout before the door opens.

Aerilyn: Selfishness

I find the courage to get out of bed and throw on my robes as I leave my room. The hallway was surprisingly empty, but just before Arabella's room, where two guards were posted. I passed them while they said nothing. I knock at her door.

"Come in," I hear her voice call out. I open the door and for the first time, I walk in her room without the courage of wine. As I close the door behind me, I see Valin and her already in here. Valin and her laying on the lounge together.

There was something warming but also heartbreaking to see it. They looked so comfortable with each other already. Like no walls were built between them. Something happy and comforting.

I walk over to them and they move just enough for me, too. I lay my head on Arabella's stomach and for a moment I felt the comforts of home. A place, something that was a fleeting feeling. I listened to the murmurs of their talking that felt drowned out my feelings. I finally sit up.

"I want to be with you both." The tone of desperation came out of me and I could feel the burning sensation. My body warning me the threats of tears but I fought them back.

"You are with us," Arabella was soft spoke in her confusion. Valin look caught my attention. He knew what I was asking, but said nothing. He looks almost like he was warning me not to. But I look back to Arabella.

I lean forward, tucking Arabella's hair behind her ear.

"No, I want to be with you both." I see the paint of flush on her cheeks as she finally realizes what I was asking.

"When I was in the cave," she looks into my eyes, fishing for the right words I didn't think I would see either of you again. I worried I would never get the chance to tell you how I felt, how I feel," she corrected. She leans her cheek into my hand and closes her eyes. "I can't help these feelings I have for you both"

I took her hand and started kissing her palm. I start to uncover her robes as she did the same for me. We mirror each other as we shake off the garments off. She is still leaning back on Valin as I lean in and start to kiss her.

There was a soft gasp as I use feather-like touches gliding over her body. Making a trail of goosebumps everywhere I touched.

Her legs fell open so easily for me as I trail my fingertips down her stomach. I look up at Valin awkwardly, not sure what to do. I take his hand and lay them on her breast. Leading the tips of his fingers to touch them lightly.

Arabella responds so sweetly. Arching and moaning with need. I go to the other and run my tongue over the other, flicking it as I felt it harden. Valins' other hand comes in and I take a few of his fingers in my mouth, running my tongue

Aerilyn: Selfishness

between the two of them. I hear him groan as he takes them out and uses my saliva to touch her nipple.

I make a trail back down her stomach. We fill the room with the smell of desire and sounds of breathless pants. I run my tongue between her folds. I feel my own pulsating need as I flick my tongue over her bud. Doing so, feeling her wither under me time and time again. Stopping right before she orgasms, denying her the release which her body begged for already.

I move and have her move with me. Leaning her back against me, running my hands down her body and making her legs spread for Valin. Putting her on full display for him.

"Come on, Valin. The princess is desperate for you. Look at how wet she is." I lazily drag two of my fingers between her folds and spread it open ever so slightly. His hand runs over his own cock, still trapped under his clothes.

"Give the good princess what she wants," I said as I kiss on her exposed neck.

"Yes, please." The two words came out like breathless pleas as she jerks her hips in my hand that continues to open her seams but only ever barely touching her clit. Her body begs for more and I continue teasing until Valin gave what she wanted.

In one movement, his shirt was off. He held my gaze as he took off his pants and strokes himself. Those dark looks I got to know that night.

"I will have to taste for myself to see if you are right." He said, challenging me. I felt my breath catch as I watch him go down on Arabella.

Arabella throws her head back on me as he went down. As I continue to tease her nipple, snaking my hand up to her neck. I hold her jaw and move her head aside so I had all the access I want to her neck. I place a kiss on the crevice and hear her cries of pleasure intensify.

"Talk to me, Princess. Does it feel good?" I nip her earlobe.

"Yes," she said with a gasp.

"Tell me how it feels." She did not say anything until I graze my teeth along her neck.

"It.." I feel my desire growing with the need to hear her confession. Valin's fingers slide in as his tongue was still busy. "It feels.."

I bite where I just kissed her, causing her to whimper.

"You were saying?"

"It feels like every part of me is alive."

"Are you ready for more?" I ask.

"Yes, please." I look down at Valin as her pleas came out.

"You heard her. She would like her pretty pussy filled." He moves with a growl of desire. He grips the back of the lounge behind me as he enters her. I kissed her skin as he met her lips. I feel him move in and out of her with slow, tortuous intent. Knowing exactly how he feels inside me.

"Princess, we need to move." He picks her and lays down on the rug. Having him ride him with her heart's content. I see the uncertainty in her eyes.

I come over, sitting behind her. I place my hands on her waist and guide her through the motions. Moving her hips along with mine as she rides him.

"Aerilyn," His husky voice almost made me cave. "Sit on my face." Moving and doing what he said, I meet Arabella in the middle and moan my pleasures into our kiss.

Arabella's movements became more. Increasing the speed, I match her rhythm. Touches and grinding between us became desperate before she starts to cry out. Strings of moans and whimpers came out of Arabella as she came. Hearing her sweet

Aerilyn: Selfishness

voice encouraging my peak to come as a crashing fall.

We moved off of Valin. She falls back as I kiss her deeply. For a moment, Valin takes my neck from behind and pulls my back against him. I turn enough to kiss him. Breaking in the heat to breathe. His pants by my ear.

"Damned Temptress." I heard him curse. I could still feel his hard length pressed against me. Leaning forward, and raise my hips for him. Giving him all the access he needs.

"Then use me," I tempt him to fuck me. I feel him open my folds as he presses his cock inside me. Arabella kisses me, muffling my moans as he slowly pushes in, but pulls out just before he enters all the way.

Continuing this for a tremendous, torturous amount of time, and I focus on the sensation alone. The slow buildup that promises another orgasm. One that what I want to take greedily.

I move, roll my hips to encourage more from him, and reach down. I start to make teasing circles around my clit. Arabella moves towards Valin. I look behind me for a second and see her taking his face for a kiss.

Valin's hold on my hips tighten and he started take more of me, faster. I feel Arabella's soft hands coming from over Valin's as she glided over to my own hands. Her fingers following the same pattern I was doing.

Moans, touches and taking so much of him was building so much want. The pulsating need to come. My own whimpers of pleasure come out as I start to clench around him, wanting every last friction.

His hand snakes around and up, leading me to sit up as he drove into me. Arabella comes around and starts kissing me. The exploration of her tongue and his increasing groans causes me to explode from my high. I could feel his own warmth spilled as we all we still from our experience.

I felt the warmth of his lips along my shoulders. Arabella letting go of my face to give him a kiss. I climb out of his lap. Laying down on the rug, Arabella nestles herself in my arms. After Valin placed a few logs in the fireplace, he grabs a blanket and taking a spot on the other side of Arabella.

He threw the blanket over up. My backside was heating well enough from the fire, but I did not plan to stay long. I felt Valin's arms snake between us and holding Arabella close.

I could not help but watch them. It looked so natural to them. The way she fit to him and him to her.

Her eyes start to drift off, leaving Valin and I staring at each other. That dull feeling slowly creeping back. The short distraction was not enough. I start to move, as Valin grabs my wrist.

"Just stay with us tonight." He wants the same as me but I couldn't. I had no place in their little world other than to be on the sideline. "Good night, Valin." I said and taking my hand back. Grabbing my clothes and I go to leave. I go without leaving a piece of me. No cup. No wine. Nothing to say I was here, but maybe in a passing memory.

I step out of the room and see Keiran talking to the guard. He looks at me and the look in his eyes says he knows what happened.

"It's over now," were the only words I could say as I leave.

Arabella: No time for goodbyes

Waking up to the blinding light of the sun peaking its way through the window, I look up and see the curtains are wide open. The feel of muscular arms around me as Valin pulls me into him tighter. I smile, loving the feel of his arms on my bare skin.

I look to where Aerilyn was last night when I last saw her before falling asleep and frown. The space was empty and the blanket on her side looks as if no one had slept there.

"Where is she?" I question, hoping he was awake. The next minute I feel the touch of his lips on my shoulder, causing goosebumps on my body. I grin, loving the feeling of his affection finally, but something inside me was shouting at me to go find Aerilyn.

"She left last night, shortly after you fell asleep," He replies and I frown, turning around to face him. He had a slight stubble on his chin and his eyes were sleepy, but his lips showing a small smile.

"And you didn't stop her?"

"I asked her to stay but you know when she has her mind made up there's no stopping her" he replies and I nod understanding where he was coming from Aerilyn was very stubborn sometimes. I lean over, grabbing the robe and wrapping it around me. Valin gives me a questioning look as I stand up.

"I'm going to check to see if she's okay," I said, moving to the closet and picking out a simple dress, one I could wear without a corset, and I know my ribs will thank me for it. I hear movement behind me and turn to see Val putting on the white shirt he had on under his outfit last night and his black pants. "What are you doing?" I smile and cross my arms.

"Coming with you, of course" His words were joking and teasing. He moves over to the door and holds it open for me. I could joke that it wasn't his job to do that anymore, but I loved his chivalry. Walking out with him, following closely behind. I wanted to hold his hand, but I also didn't want to push him too soon. The halls were bustling with maids and workers, each nodding their heads in respect to us.

The moment we reached Aerilyn's door, something felt off to me. Nervously, I knock on the door and wait for a reply. Nothing. I twist the doorknob and the door opens with ease. I walk into the room and notice everything is clean and not just clean, the room is empty apart from the furniture inside.

My body froze. It was almost as if I knew this was going to happen. I didn't know exactly where she is but something inside me just understood that she was gone and not coming back.

Thank you. The words hitting me from our conversation before the wedding. *Was she saying goodbye to me?* I could see Valin walk around the room looking for her. I knew he had hoped that she had simply just switched rooms. He inspects

Arabella: No time for goodbyes

every inch of the room as I place my hand on the back of the couch to steady myself. I was almost having an out-of-body experience. I hear Valin's footsteps rush out to the door, turning my head to look towards him. He was looking left and right as if he was looking for a servant.

"Excuse me, do you know where the duchess is?" Val questions. A servant comes into my view. I walk over to them, my legs feeling shaking as if they would give way any moment.

"Not quite. The duchess has taken off across the seas. I'm not sure exactly where," the servant replied. My throat tightened and I couldn't speak. Val looks shocked, angry and upset all in one.

"What do you mean overseas? Why would she just leave without saying anything!?" Val's voice raises and the servant steps back in fear.

"I don't know, your highness, someone mentioned she was to marry Sir Keiran, and they went to marry." He rambles. Val let the servant go, and he hurries away. Val turns to face me and that was when I lost it.

"No" I shake my head as my bottom lip quivers as my heart almost shatters. The tears fall down my cheeks as my legs give up and I drop to the floor. I sit on the ground and I sob so hard that I could feel myself catching my breath. Val kneels in front of me, his eyes wet with tears. He brings me close to him and my face was in his chest, my tears wetting his shirt.

"Arabella, I need you to breathe, okay? Grieve but please breathe," He says lifting my head up with his hands. His thumbs rub my cheeks. I look into his eyes and I see him crying, too. He was consoling me but he was grieving too. He had feelings for her just as I do and yet he pushes that away to get me to breathe. I calm my breathing down, but the tears don't stop.

"Why would she leave and not say goodbye? She didn't say anything, she just left."

"I don't know. Maybe she just didn't want to have to say goodbye or maybe she didn't want us to stop her," He says wiping his cheeks.

"Do you think she will come back to us?" I ask, feeling useless both for me and for him.

"I don't know Arabella. I hope so. One day we will see her again" He says but his words sound as if it was something he was hoping for to.

I close my eyes and pray for the words in my head find their way to wherever she is.

"Aerilyn, I love you"

Aerilyn's Father

I rode in the carriage with Aerilyn to the boat. There were no words exchanged between us, but then again, what was I supposed to say? I haven't been able to hold a conversation since her mother passed. She was my light and felt the fire dissipate with her final breath.

Aerilyn sat on the other side of the carriage, just staring out the window. I knew she was mad at me, but this was for her own good. She needs to get off this island. Even more so when she went missing, only to come back with the princess. There were things in motion. If I could get her to the other side of the world, I would. This was the best I could offer.

There was a fire in her eyes which matched her mother and had to be hidden. As the days passed, the more she looked and acted like her.

The smell of the salty sea water became stronger and I could hear the call of seabirds. The carriage stops moving, and the door opens. She walks out, and I follow her. She stands there just staring at the boat. I waited for the tears, pleading something, but she just turns around and hugs me.

I stand there for a moment before wrapping my arms around her. Thinking back, I don't remember the last time I had embraced my little girl, but she was no little girl anymore. I hold back the tears that were threatening to come.

She pulls back with a somber look. Placing a hand on my cheek, she leans up and places a kiss on my cheek.

"I love you Father." She whispered and left.

I watch her get on that boat after touching my cheek. Never once turning around. Never once telling me off. Never once.

Bonus: Arabella: Heart Desires

Rewrite the stars - Anne Marie and James Arthur

Not something canon for the story but a fun POV that was written for the story if it fit. Enjoy!

I lay my head in Aerilyn's lap as her soft fingers stroke my hair affectionately. She smiles down at me and I smile up at her.

"Can I ask you something?" I ask. She nods *yes,* waiting for my question. "Do you ever wish you could be somebody else?" Her fingers stop stroking my hair momentarily.

"Sometimes maybe, did something happen Arabella?" She questions, her face showing with worry.

"A few weeks ago I had a talk with my father about going out into the town and visit the people, show them that I care and that I am worthy of being a princess. He denied me, of course, and part of me hates him for it, but the other part of me understands why he did it. But being in this castle always being watched what I'm doing, if I walk into a room the staff stop talking and quickly stand straight, I am in a palace surrounded by gates I feel like I'm in some form of jail, I feel trapped," I express. A tear escapes and fell down my cheek, but Aerilyn quickly caught it with her finger.

"I'm sorry, I wish I could help somehow," she says to me and kisses my forehead.

I sigh and enjoy the sensation of her lips on my forehead.

"Maybe I should tell him I will not take the crown, that them finding a new person to take the throne will be the better option. Then you can take me away from this town." I joke.

"Do you really want that?" She asks me, staring at my lips and then my eyes. I gulp my cheeks, heating just from her gaze. She leaned forward. Her lips were close to mine.

"Do you really want to give up on your people?" She questions, and as much as I wanted to say the word 'yes' to her and carry on being the daughter my father wants me to be, I couldn't lie to her.

"No" I say and lean up pressing my lips to hers it was a soft and passionate kiss at first but the desperation I felt for her intensified the moment I slowly sit up and meet my lips back with hers, her back was now resting against the headboard and she was letting me do what I wanted, she was giving me the power I so desperately needed right now.

I lift her nightgown over her head and look down to see she wasn't wearing any undergarments underneath; I bite my bottom lip, staring at her breasts. Running my fingertips over her hard nipples, her chest was rising up and down deep. I look back at her eyes to see her intently staring at me.

Bonus: Arabella: Heart Desires

"Arabella, you don't have to do anything you're not comfortable with," she whispers. Her hand moves to rest on my cheek and I lean into it for a moment.

"I'm comfortable Aerilyn, I've always been comfortable around you." I say and lean forward, placing our lips back together. My hand moves back to her right breast and at the initial contact, I hear her moan. Smiling, knowing she is as affected just like me, I move my kisses down her jaw to her neck. My lips move down to each of her breasts. I grab one softly and my mouth sucks on her nipple. Her moans fill the room, giving me confidence that I was doing this correctly.

I move further down, trailing my kisses down her stomach. My lips kiss her upper thigh as I spread her legs open.

I lean forward so I was lay on my stomach in front of her. My hand moving forward, rubbing circles on her sensitive clit. Her moans were like euphoria to me, urging me to go further. I licked up her already wet slit, my fingers still rubbing circles. She moans my name, and that was the encouragement I needed. My tongue thrusts into her folds and I start moving it in and out of her. Her hips grinds, matching my thrusts with her own. We were two people giving into the temptations and letting our desire take over.

I move my mouth up to her clit and suck on it. Aerilyn's hand moves into my hair, moving it out of my face. Her body starts to shake and with her release, she moans a sweet prayer to the gods.

I roll over to lie next to her, looking at her. I interlock our hands together and I stare at them before looking up at her.

"Will you stay with me tonight?" I ask her. The fear of being alone was killing me tonight. She smiles back at me and nods.

"Of course, you would have to order me to leave for me to

leave you tonight," she says, causing me to giggle. I lay my head on her chest, slowly closing my eyes as she draws circles on my back soothingly.

But I couldn't help but worry about how much I need this woman, how much I felt for her.

Printed in Great Britain
by Amazon